P9-EGN-723

The Story of Hercules

BOB BLAISDELL

Illustrated by Thea Kliros

DOVER PUBLICATIONS, INC.
Mineola, New York

DOVER CHILDREN'S THRIFT CLASSICS
EDITOR OF THIS VOLUME: SUSAN L. RATTINER

Dedication

To my children, Max and Odette
B. B.

Published in Canada by General Publishing Company, Ltd., 30 Lesmill Road, Don Mills, Toronto, Ontario.
Published in the United Kingdom by Constable and Company, Ltd., 3 The Lanchesters, 162–164 Fulham Palace Road, London W6 9ER.

Bibliographical Note

The Story of Hercules, first published by Dover Publications, Inc., in 1997, is a new adaptation, by Bob Blaisdell, of the legends of Hercules. The illustrations have also been prepared specially for the present edition.

Library of Congress Cataloging-in-Publication Data

Blaisdell, Robert.
    The story of Hercules / Bob Blaisdell ; illustrated by Thea Kliros.
        p.   cm.—(Dover children's thrift classics)
    Summary: An adaptation of the legend of Hercules, son of the god Zeus and a mortal woman and renowned for his great strength, who performs twelve "impossible" tasks.
    ISBN 0-486-29768-3 (pbk.)
    1. Heracles (Greek mythology)—Juvenile literature. 2. Hercules (Roman mythology)—Juvenile literature. [1. Heracles (Greek mythology) 2. Hercules (Roman mythology) 3. Mythology, Greek. 4. Mythology, Roman.] I. Kliros, Thea, ill. II. Title. III. Series.
BL820.H5B53   1997
398.2'0938'02—dc21   97–11715
                                                             CIP
                                                             AC

Manufactured in the United States of America
Dover Publications, Inc., 31 East 2nd Street, Mineola, N.Y. 11501

Contents

She pleaded, her hands clasped in prayer, whispering, "Great Zeus, let my husband's mission be fulfilled, and return him to me."

1. My Birth, Childhood and Youth

I AM the Greek hero Hercules, son of lord god Zeus and earth-dwelling mortal Alcmene. I earned the privilege to live with the gods on heavenly Mount Olympos through performing nearly impossible labors, tasks assigned to me because of jealous Hera, Zeus's divine queen.

Let me tell you the tale of my tremendous deeds, of my heroic accomplishments, of my terrible, overwhelming sorrows and stupid mistakes. For I, like all beings, was born with faults, the chief of which was a fiery temper.

Before my birth, my mother and her husband, Amphitryon, left their native city of Tiryns in the Peloponnese and found a home in the kingdom of Thebes. Shortly after their arrival, however, Amphitryon set out on a dangerous expedition. When my mother entered Zeus's temple to pray for Amphitryon's safe return, Zeus observed her and fell in love, for he believed her the most beautiful mortal woman he had ever seen. She wore her hair with a black ribbon, tying it back from her lustrous forehead, and her large eyes were nearly as soft and gentle as those of a newborn deer. She pleaded, her hands clasped in prayer, whispering, "Great Zeus, let my husband's mission be fulfilled, and return him to me, his loving bride."

Zeus answered her prayer, it is true, but not before he himself, that very night, came down from the heavens in a carriage borne by immortal winged horses. By taking on the resemblance of good Amphitryon he tricked my mother into accepting him into her arms. The result of their embraces, in nine months' time, was myself.

Not until the night after his visit did Zeus allow Amphitryon to return. My mother gave birth to Iphicles, my half-brother, a few minutes after my delivery. Amphitryon knew that I was Zeus's son, not his own, but he loved me as well as any father could.

Before my birth, however, great Zeus made the mistake of boasting of my conception. He declared before the other gods upon Olympos that the next-born descendant of Perseus, my great-grandfather, and one of Zeus's earlier mortal sons, would become the king of Tiryns. Hera, resenting Zeus's ambitions for me, called on the goddess of childbirth to delay my mother's delivery and to bring on the early birth of Eurystheus, another descendant of noble Perseus.

These acts of Hera's enraged Zeus, but what could he do? He himself had made his word law, and so Eurystheus inherited the throne, and I, as you shall soon hear, was eventually made his slave.

Even as a baby I displayed fearlessness and strength, much to my mother's pride. Even in her very old age, she enjoyed telling the story of a night when my half-brother Iphicles and I were eight months old, and she awoke, hearing a hissing sound from our room. She got up to check on us, and when she entered the doorway with a lighted candle, she gasped, then screamed out for Amphitryon. As she watched in horror, I sat up in my crib, my strong little hands gripping two fork-tongued snakes by the throat. She says I smiled at the sight of her, and that I laughed as I waved the limp bodies of the poisonous serpents I had strangled.

When I was still a boy, Amphitryon taught me how to

As she watched in horror, I sat up in my crib,
gripping two fork-tongued snakes by the throat.

drive a chariot. We were on a plain, almost bare of trees, with fine roads. "Hold the reins just so," he warned me, "and if you feel the horses pull too hard, hand the reins up to me, and I'll take over."

"I believe, good father" (he allowed me to call him so), "that these horses will do what I instruct them to do."

Thunder and Lightning were the names of the hot-tempered, almost untamed horses. Upon seeing their usual master hand over the reins to a little curly-haired boy, they snorted, as if insulted that Amphitryon believed I could possibly control them. They broke forward, jolting the chariot and sending Amphitryon head over heels and into the dust behind the chariot. I was alone in the hard-wheeled chariot as it bounced along, threatening to tip over.

Believe it or not, I was enjoying my solo with the reins. Wicked Lightning, the more feisty horse, glanced over his shoulder to see what it was that was tugging at its reins, for he believed I had long since been bounced out of the chariot. In spite of having been thrown to the floor of the chariot, I had held on to the reins with my fists. Finally I pulled myself to my feet, and once I had done so the horses became aware of who was master. I reined them in, controlling their wild actions, and then as they snorted with rage and surprise and began running in step and straight ahead, I lashed them with the spare ends of the reins, shouting at them, "So it's speed you want? Let's see just how fast you can go!"

Amphitryon had, by this time, picked himself up from the dust and saddled another horse, and was giving us chase. I saw him in the distance, and to prove my mastery to my teacher, I directed the horses in tighter and tighter loops.

Amphitryon reined in his mare and watched in amazement as I circled closer and closer to him, till the horses staggered and came to an exhausted halt.

"Hercules," he called out, "you are more than a match for the finest horses in Thebes. If you were older, you could be charioteer for any general."

"Why not now?" I asked, laughing.

"Because," said Amphitryon, "there are other skills you should learn. I was sure I was starting you too young for this, but now I see you've long been ready to become a hero among men."

Modesty is not a trait that I value, and so I must mention my early achievements and successes. From Eurytos I quickly learned to shoot a bow; from the thief Autolycos, expert at cunning moves, I learned to wrestle; from marvelous Mudrikion to hurl the spear; from Castor to use a sword. I was a master of all the fighting arts while still a boy. Castor claimed that by the age of seventeen I was the best fighter who ever lived.

What I lack in modesty, I hope to make up for in honesty, and so I shall have to tell of my failure in the art of music.

My one disappointed teacher was Linus, brother of famous Orpheus, that creator of songs so powerful and affecting that even objects like trees and stones were moved to follow him, and wicked men with stony hearts were made to weep. Linus was nearly the equal of his brother, and he came to Thebes to see if I could be the prodigy in music I already was in warfare. Alas, no.

Linus was not at all awed by my strength, poor man, and he treated me as if I were just any old student. When I played the lyre poorly, he scolded me.

"Music requires feeling, not strength," he said. Even then, as a lad of seventeen, I knew the truth of his words, but I hated the shame he brought to my reddened face when he pointed out my awkward fingerings on the strings, or when he said with disgust, "Music! *Music!* Not power!" But he forgot himself, or should I say he forgot who *I* was—even then the strongest man alive.

He had seen how sensitively and accurately I could pluck the string of a bow to shoot an arrow when I saw an angry beast in the distance. He knew that I was more than just a young man of strength, that my power came to me through perception, wits and strategy. I admit, yes, my music skills were meager, but he need not have shamed me and made me so aware of my deficiencies. He should not have used my other skills to belittle me for the one that eluded me.

One day as I plucked away at the childish tune he had painstakingly taught me, I became distracted. Outside the garden where Linus gave me lessons I observed a hare hopping in the meadow.

Even today I remember the rude way the rabbit flashed its tail at me, as if it knew I was helpless to give it chase. Its black eye winked at me, and I longed to put away the lyre once and for all.

Linus saw my distraction; more importantly he heard my fumbling fingers distort the simple melody. I did not see but suddenly felt the back of his hand slap me across the face. Believe me, he saw the shock and shame in my unbearded cheeks and innocent eyes. Even so, he was used to students who would put up with such indignities. I kept myself and my anger under control until he said, "That should help you, stupid boy, to keep your mind from wandering."

I jumped to my feet. Imagine a little dog yapping and nipping at a lion. Just so was it with Linus slapping at me. Though I meant to storm away, I saw his hand rise in preparation for another slap.

I struck him with my lyre, knocking him to the ground. Then I continued on my way, out of the garden and across the meadow after that hare. I could not, however, seem to take any pleasure in the hunt, and after several minutes I returned to the palace, moping.

My mother immediately noticed my dark mood and the damaged lyre that hung over my shoulder.

"Poor Hercules," she said.

"I am very angry at Linus," I said. "I refuse to continue my music lessons." I was ashamed before her, because I had wished to be able to please her with my talent in music, to play gentle songs that would amuse her. I had failed.

What is more, within the hour we received the news that Linus, that weak old man who had provoked my fierce temper, had died as a result of the blow I had given him! What a monster I seemed to myself! Yet neither my mother nor Amphitryon wholly blamed me when they heard of Linus' treatment of me. Even so, Amphitryon advised me that my education at home was over, that I must set out into the world and there learn the hard lessons of experience.

2. I Go into the World

TO TRY to redeem myself in the eyes of my family and country, I set out in pursuit of the ravaging lion that was attacking the cattle of Amphitryon and our neighbor, King Thespios. This lion had a stronger taste for death than for food. If he found a herd of thirty, he killed them all, but ate only one or two. And the next day he looked for more herds. He enjoyed, it seemed, killing men, for he attacked shepherds and cowherds at any opportunity he found, undeterred by their spears or arrows. Even with paid hunters, Amphitryon and King Thespios could not capture it. At best they kept it at bay for a day or two.

With my bow and arrows and spear, I bade farewell to my weeping mother, announcing at the same time my intention of killing the lion. Alcmene, my sweet mother, caressed my curly mop of hair and her eyes were shiny with tears. I admit that her tears almost brought on mine.

"My dear son," she said, "do not try anything so dangerous. Please go with your brother Iphicles and Amphitryon. No one doubts your courage or strength. But use reason and live a long life. Yours has had such a remarkable beginning!"

I smiled at her words, pleased with her love, but I answered, "Mother, you'll soon see me, not laid out for a funeral, but decked in glory."

I hiked off to a rich green pasture, where Amphitryon kept the finest of his cattle. Their horns were plated

7

with gold, their hides were lustrous, cared for by many servants. Their meat was reserved as gifts for kings and princes; their milk for our own family. These cattle, a herd of forty, I led out of the pasture, in spite of the objections of Jervinios, their chief caretaker.

"Your father's prize beefers! Please, good Hercules, do not expose them to danger! They are safe here!"

"Jervinios, kindly, loyal friend, do not worry. You'll see them all safe and sound tomorrow."

I made good on my word. The lion must have been proud of how he could elude trained hunters and trackers, but how could he resist attacking a lone boy and the finest, most tempting cattle in the land? I led the creatures into the open meadows beside the mountainside. From high above us the surprised lion roared with pleasure. No fool, when he arrived in the meadow he made a complete circle of us, looking for a trap. Seeing none, and overcome by intense longing, that evening he came crawling through the grass towards me at my fire. I pretended not to notice, even though the cattle, their fear overtaking them, fled to the far side of the meadow, where they lowed in dread.

When I sensed the lion within striking distance, I stood up, only at that moment deciding to use my spear rather than bow. The lion rose to its feet and snarled. The next moment its roar deafened me, but I did not flinch. He took two bounds and then leapt with his claws out and fangs bared. I was about to pitch my spear at him when he knocked it from my hands, landing on me. His face fell toward mine, but I grabbed his chest and used my feet to propel him over my shoulders. He landed in a heap, stunned. I picked up my spear and cocked it for a fatal throw, but he bounded to his feet, and, like a cowardly dog, his tail between his

*I grabbed the lion's chest and used my feet
to propel him over my shoulders.*

legs, began to run away. I ran after and jumped upon
him, tackling him by his back legs, and we wrestled.

Picture this: the crown of his shaggy head forced
down against my chest, my chin digging into his skull,
his right hind leg struggling to keep on the ground; his
left leg pushing off my thigh, his forepaws pushing off
against my chest, my brawny arms joined around his
back. Both of us were grunting out terrible roars as we
struggled to the death. Finally, and now you will understand my astounding strength, I flexed my arms once,
tightly, and the beast gasped out its last breath, then
fell as limp as a bundle of linen.

That night I slept by the fire, and in the morning,
pulling the lion's carcass by the tail, I walked home,
driving the cattle before me. At the sight of me and my
prize there was never such joy expressed as that by

Alcmene, nor more amazement than that expressed by Amphitryon.

Let me return our attention to jealous Hera. She had not forgiven Zeus for my creation, nor did she like the watchful loving kindness he had for me. Zeus knew of my many youthful triumphs. Since Hera had thwarted his wishes for my kingship, he wanted me to one day join the gods and live as an immortal. This did not suit Hera. As it was later recounted to me by wise goddess Athene, Zeus's plans for me became a matter of heated debate.

"Hercules is the mortal of all mortals," declared Zeus to a counsel of gods. "As such, I mean for him to live with us after his mortal days are done." The lord god looked round, from one face to another, all of them but one nodding to his wish. Not Hera. With any married couple, there is disagreement. "Well?" thundered Zeus, knowing there would be a fight. "Well, why not?"

Hera, queen of all goddesses, gave my father a look that seemed to mean, "Surely you must be joking!" Finally, with all the gods awaiting her reply, she said, "A puny mortal!"

"He's not puny!"

"Born," she went on, disregarding my father, but making her case to her fellow divinities, "born of a human . . . *creature!*"

Zeus's heavy brow grew heavier, and he scowled. Have you seen black clouds gathering on a mountain range? Just so must have been my father's appearance. Yet Zeus, the greatest of gods, unconquerable by Titans or Giants, was conquered by a jealous sulk. He did not burst out in fury, but checked himself and said, "It is my wish that he become a god."

"Why not, then, dirty our waters with all of the mortal children we gods have produced?" replied Hera.

"This Hercules," rumbled Zeus, "is the one I have chosen. He is the only one worthy of us, the only one capable of assisting us in our future battle with the Giants, those monsters, unleashed by Gaia the Earth mother. They wish to depose us from our thrones. Granted, this battle is several years away, but where or how would we find another mortal so ready and able? Remember, the signs we saw in the stars tell us that we will need the assistance of a mortal in that fight."

Hera smiled, a dangerous response, since she is a calculating, humorless queen. "I take your point, Lord Zeus," she said. "But because we set such store by this boy of yours, shouldn't we try him out?"

"Try him out!" exclaimed Zeus, his hands gripping the arms of his throne. "Try him out!"

"Precisely, my lord."

"How? Where? Why?"

"Require him over the period of a dozen years to serve his cousin, King Eurystheus, and perform a few— say, ten—chores worthy of a god."

Zeus was about to refuse, but he saw the agreement and sympathy with Hera's proposal in the expressions of the other gods. Perhaps, he thought, he could enlist his daughter Athene to aid Hercules. And the instant he had such a thought, Athene, wisest of all goddesses, understood, and, so she tells me, she touched her father's elbow, and nodded at him. Zeus seemed pleased then, and turned to Hera, saying, "Very well."

"Shall we then dispatch swift Hermes to the boy and inform him of his opportunity?" asked Hera.

"Do not allow Eurystheus to overburden Hercules, wife."

"Of course not," said Hera.

Within moments of this dawn meeting upon Olympos, I sat up from my blanket. I was beside a cold

Then a handsome, godly young man appeared,
sending chills down my spine.

firepit on the bank of a narrow stream. I was on my way into the world, with no aim but discovery. Then a handsome, godly young man appeared, standing across the stream from me.

The sight of monsters would scarcely have daunted me at the time, but the sight of this young man sent chills down my spine. I knew, despite his unassuming appearance, that he was a god. I bowed my head, and in the next moment he stood before me, lifting my chin with his fingers.

"I come to you, Hercules, with an offer from the gods on Olympos, an offer approved by your father, Lord Zeus. If you wish to live as an immortal, you must first serve Eurystheus——"

"That scoundrel!" I exclaimed.

"You must serve him and perform any ten labors he assigns you," he continued. "Should you survive the labors and succeed, the gods, not Death, shall greet you at the termination of your earthly life."

Had I known the terrors I was soon to face—the monsters, the years of agony, the journey to Hades—would I have accepted? Thankfully, mortal men cannot see the future, or many of them would turn from their doors, fall back into their beds and not come out from under the covers again.

I, in blissful ignorance, readily agreed to the gods' offer. And after all is said and done, I am glad that I did. For here on Olympos I live forever, and my tale of earthbound accomplishments, namely the Labors of Hercules, is known throughout the world.

3. My First Labor: To Kill the Nemean Lion

BEFORE THE day of the gods' offer was over, I was in Tiryns, a port city near Mycenae, on that southern peninsula of mainland Greece, the Peloponnese. I went to Eurystheus' palace to await his orders.

Remember that he was my cousin, whose birth had preceded my own, thus giving him the Tirynian throne Zeus had meant for me. Hera's deviousness had taken the throne away from me, and just before I announced my presence to Eurystheus, she descended to earth to goad him on: "Do not be taken in by Hercules' boldness or beauty or his seeming frankness. He is a sly one!" she told him. She appeared to him in the guise of Tervalonios, a white-bearded sage. "Zeus's son means to steal your throne," she said. "For the next dozen years you have him at your command to perform ten duties. He is a lion-killer, so do not let him survive or he shall surely murder you."

Even Eurystheus recognized a god when he saw one, and he tremblingly told the goddess in disguise, "Whoever you are, whatever you say, I understand and will comply. I shall rid myself and the world of my cousin in short order."

I entered the throne room just as Tervalonios turned into a sparrow and flew off into the heavens. This was not a good sign for me. Eurystheus looked at me with fear and hate, but was silent. He scratched his chin, and for several minutes sat wrapped in a cloak of thought. Finally he spoke: "You agree to serve me, to perform ten tasks, whatever they may be, and just as I say?"

"Yes."

He got up and walked toward me, surveying me up and down, walking around me, and snorting with mockery. "I have heard you were lucky enough to kill a lion," he remarked.

The fool! Never could he have killed a mouse without fainting. All his power lay in his position, while all mine lay in my wits and strength.

"Let us say, cousin," he went on, "that your first task will suit your lionish tastes. Go kill the lion of Nemea."

Nemea was many miles off. I was armed with bow and arrows, a knife and a spear. Yet I feared nothing and believed, rather, that this Nemean lion would flee at seeing me.

When I arrived in Nemea, however, I learned this was no ordinary lion I was to challenge. He was the freakish offspring of the monsters Echidna and Typhon. I was told the lion was lying at rest in its cave after days of marauding. No fence had ever held it back, so splendid a leaper was he. He had made Nemea a barren land— the number of livestock had dwindled to nearly nothing. The lion would sniff out his prey and attack, no matter how many men were there to protect the sheep or goats or cattle or pheasants. He killed the animals and killed the men who tended them. They had shot arrows at him, thrown spears at him, but he never turned away.

Finding my way to his cave on his hillside, I called out, "Lion, beast of destruction, you have met your match."

I clanged the edge of my spearhead against the boulder beside the entry. The iron rang and for the next several moments I expected the lion's charge. Lucky for me he was lazily enjoying the food in his stomach and refused to budge. All I could see from the entry was the blinking of yellow eyes. "Come on out!" I shouted. I waited another several moments before stepping into the cave. I saw no eyes now; instead, I heard a sawing roar. In the dark cave I could see nothing, yet the snoring—for this is what it was—could have brought me to the lion's mouth, yet I refused to attack a sleeping enemy. So loud was his snoring the lion could not have heard my challenge had I shouted in his ears. I retreated and walked down the hill until I found a dwelling.

An old woman was sitting outside a low, tumble-down shack. She was on a stool, by a fire, cooking a stew in a pot.

"Good afternoon, granny," I said.

"To them's that don't live 'round here, I'll wager it's a fine enough day," she said. She looked at me and nodded. "But have a sit-down, sonny, and tell me wheres you're headed."

"I mean to return to the den where the lion sleeps and rouse him to a fight," I said.

"I hadn't taken you for a *fool*," said the old woman. "I guesses now I could be just as wrong as anybody else."

"Before morning, with your help, the lion will be dead."

"What?" cackled the old woman. "Are you going to feed him my carcass and hope he chokes on my brittle old bones?" She laughed at this so much she began to cough, and I had to gently pat her on the back. "Thankee, sonny," she said.

"Just a touch of your fire is all I ask, granny. I mean to smoke the monster out of his cave, so I may have the chance to stab him with my spear."

She suddenly became grim. "Young man, I like you." She struck me on the arm and said, "If I was young, I'd flirt with you. So let me tell you this, you *are* a fool."

"Is it your habit to call bravery foolishness?" I asked.

"No, I calls foolishness foolishness. It is as it does, don't you know? Didn't no one never tell you that lion has skin that nothing can't get through? Arrows, stones, knives, spears, sticks—they've all been tried. The lion no more cares for such pricks than a man like you minds a mosquito bite—less even! 'Cause a skeeter will draw your blood, but no arrows of yours will show you the red of that beast's blood. I tells you this 'cause I seen my own husband and sons try to destroy the creature that's destroyed this land. I'm an old woman, with nothing to eat but thistles seasoned with the salt of my tears, but I wouldn't like to see you go and get eated up by that demon lion."

What spirited young man has ever heeded the wise words of his elders? No, her words inflamed me to avenge the deaths of her husband and children, to see if my weapons would succeed where others had failed.

I borrowed a smoky piece of charred wood from her fire, bade her farewell, and told her that I would stop by on my way back to Tiryns and bring her something good to eat. She wept tears into her pot of stew, then shouted after me again about my foolishness.

In the twilight I called to the beast to come out and face me, but there was no reply, only that terrible snoring. So I chopped down a tree and with a knife fashioned what became my favorite weapon, a hearty, simple, knotted club.

Then I made a fire, piling on green branches after it began to dance with high flames, and fanned the smoke into the cave. The snoring died down, replaced by a thunderous coughing. Spear ready, I awaited the lion's attack. I have never quaked in my sandals, but in recollection I can hardly comprehend why I did not do so at this moment. The lion was furious, his eyes flashing, his mouth wide, roaring for my flesh. He was twice, no, thrice the size of the previous lion I had defeated. I planted my feet and launched the spear with all my strength.

Try this: take a pine needle, green and sharp or even brown and stiff, and drop it on a stone. Does the stone crumble, does the needle so much as stick in the surface? It was just so when my spear met the chest of that lion. I began to fear that what the old woman had said was true, that the hide of the beast was impenetrable. Nevertheless, there over my shoulder hung my quiver of arrows, and instantly I let loose one arrow after another, the lion not even troubling to brush them away. I hurled my new club at him; it bounced away. Finally he rushed at me and made a leap. I ducked under him, falling to my back and grasped hold of his chest. He landed roughly upon me: my life was certainly at its end!

I reached up through his curly mane and pressed my thumbs into his throat. My fingers on each hand were desperate to meet each other. I tightened my grip as I lifted myself to my feet. Again, as with the previous lion, I managed to press his head down against my chest, my chin bearing down on his crown. My hands lost hold of his massive throat and slipped till they caught hold behind his back. I grasped my hands together and pulled him into a fatal embrace—how many minutes was it before I cracked his back in two!

It was night by this time. I dropped beside the conquered beast and slept until morning.

It was rosy-fingered Dawn that woke me. I remembered my promise to the old woman and quickly collected my arrows and spear, all of whose tips were blunted by the lion's thick hide, and retrieved my sturdy club, not much the worse for wear. I was thinking I would chase down a rabbit or two. I prayed to Lord

*I grasped my hands together and pulled the
Nemean lion into a fatal embrace.*

Zeus, giving him thanks for the strength and courage with which he had blessed me.

Then, as if to spare me further trouble, Zeus blessed me with the sight of a sheep lying in the dark cave. Its neck was broken, undoubtedly by a quick blow from the Nemean lion the night before; otherwise, however, it was untouched.

I picked up this sheep and flung her over one shoulder, while over the other I towed by its tail the immense, weighty carcass of the lion. I marched across the countryside with my prizes, and in honor of my success composed a little song:

> Has there been a finer hero on the loose
> Whose father was the god we call great Zeus?
> Greater than Hercules?
> Fall on your knees!
> For my name is Hercules, defeater of the Nemean lion,
> I'm hungry as an ox or sheep—which I'll soon be fryin'.

Linus, had he lived, would have mocked me, and god Apollo, patron of the arts, must have laughed at my silly song; but I could not resist singing in my own honor, so full of pride was I.

From a long distance, out of my hearing anyway, the old woman took notice of my approach. Though she was none too spry, she began dancing with hops and leaps around her little fire. The first words I heard were: "You foolish boy!" But she was smiling and clearly overjoyed, for she saw me dragging not only the lion but the sheep.

When I arrived at her fire, she hopped up to me and touched my cheeks with her old hands, laughed, and said, "The gods must be in your corner, sonny-boy, I tells you that."

When I was about to skin and prepare the lamb for cooking, she said, "Oh, you let me take cares of the cookin'. In the meantime, you get down off your big feets and tell me the story of that there lion."

"That I will, granny." And so I told her what I have told you, only I was distracted as I spoke, for an idea, like fine mist, was falling upon me. "Granny," I said, "why should I drag this lion all the way to Tiryns?"

"Why should you?" she answered. "'Cause if you don't, no one'll take your word you killed him. There's gots to be proof, Herky."

"Wouldn't the skin be proof enough?"

"'Course it would . . . if you had something that'd cut that tough hide—which, I gotta reminds you, you don't have."

"But perhaps I do," I answered.

While the old woman quoted her own words at me, about how neither metal, nor wood, nor stone could penetrate the lion's hide, I knelt beside the carcass and lifted one of its paws. Had I a sword or knife as sharp as this lion's claws, no man would have ever dared to challenge me to fight. I grasped one digit of that massive claw, and poked it at the lion's chest. There was a cut! In no time, I skinned the lion using his own claws.

The old woman came from a family of tanners, and she helped me prepare the lion skin so that I would be able to wear it as a robe. We stretched it on pegs, drying it in the hot sun, and scraping it clean in front and back. The skinless carcass we left in a pit a good distance away, and day after day the birds of prey flew from miles and lands away to pick at it until there was nothing left but bones.

A sweeter companion I have never known than the old woman, Trisia, and we spent a good month or two in conversation. My only duty was to fetch her fish and game, which she cooked each day while I told her my stories and she told me hers.

There I stood, in my great height and massive brawn, my big face peering out through the jaws of the lion.

When, finally, the lion skin was ready to wear, I put it on one morning, nearly scaring poor Trisia out of her wits.

There I stood, in my great height and massive brawn, my big face peering out through my new helmet, the jaws of the lion; the forepaws tied at my chest, the back legs falling at my sides and the tail almost trailing on the ground.

"Oh, lordy!" Trisia exclaimed. "I thought for a moment the lion skin had come back to life and grabbed you and eated you up!" Then, with tears in her eyes, she bade me a fond farewell.

Was Eurystheus pleased to see me? Perhaps I should have warned him of my return. Seeing a man wrapped in a cloak of lion skin, he leaped out of his throne and into a large jar.

"Guards!" he shouted. "Oh, guards! The lion I sent Hercules to kill has killed and eaten him!"

I stood, arms folded, peering out at him from between the jaws of the Nemean lion. "As you bid, king, I have done," I said.

The guards had not dared to approach me, though none of them were silly enough to take me for the lion. They saw me and knew me as the hero Hercules.

Eurystheus got up the courage to take a long look at me from the lip of the jar. Then he climbed out, brushed the dust from his knees and elbows and reseated himself on the throne. "I knew it was you all along, Hercules. But I had been napping, and I was confused, thinking I saw a live lion."

"The Nemean lion is dead, and I wear his skin as my trophy," I declared.

"Yes," said Eurystheus, "though it's not at all becoming on you. That labor must have been easier than I imagined. In fact, I should have done it myself. But this next one, I promise, won't be so easy! I command you, you brute, to do away with the most horrible monster that has ever plagued mankind, the hydra of Lerna, that famous nine-headed snake monster!"

I thought Eurystheus "the most horrible monster that has ever plagued mankind," but I said nothing, only nodded and left the palace.

4. I Meet Iolaos, and Do Two Labors, but Get Credit for Only One

BEFORE I ventured to Lerna, I visited with my half-brother, Iphicles, who, wretched man, had come willingly, even on his knees, to Eurystheus' service and lived in his palace. There was a young, handsome boy in Iphicles' charge, the brother of his wife, Automedusa. There was a boldness and seeming fearlessness in the eyes of twelve-year-old Iolaos. My brother disliked him, thought him trouble, and kept trying to drive him from the room as we talked.

"Let him be, Iphicles. I like the lad," I said. Sometimes a first impression tells all—and I owe my life to this first impression, as Iolaos became my greatest mortal ally.

Iphicles said, "Very well! Like him as much as you want. Though Eurystheus would have me killed for saying so, I advise you to give up this path you are on. Immortality is not for mortals—Eurystheus' labors will kill you. How do you expect, in any case, to defeat such a monster as the hydra?"

"Uncle Hercules!" cried Iolaos, "let me go fight the hydra with you! To die fighting beside you would be honorable and glorious!"

I laughed! This from a mere boy, while men twice his size and age quaked in their shoes at the mention of the hydra. Seeing his eyes grow misty at my laughter, however, I patted Iolaos on the head and told him, "You do me honor, lad. In fact, you remind me of myself when I was your age—I was also eager to face danger."

"Let me come with you!" the boy pleaded. Iphicles, irritated at this request, grabbed at the boy's cloak in order to fling him from the room.

Iolaos jumped away, as if a snake had struck at him, and he stared defiantly at his sister's husband.

Before a fight could occur, I stood up and escorted Iolaos from the room. Iphicles was shouting after us that we were knuckleheads, both of us, and that he didn't care if we ended up being supper for the hydra. I had no intention, however, of taking Iolaos along with me.

But as we stood outside, under the night sky, we watched a star streak across the blue dome of the heavens, and yet it did not disappear, as other shooting stars do. We saw its sparkling light drop toward us. There was a blinding flash before us, and in the next instant, when our eyes cleared, there stood the god Hermes. From his shiny gold cloak he pulled out a huge, gleaming shield and a long sword, and he presented them to me as a fisherman would offer another man a prize fish—two hands outstretched, nodding and smiling. I thanked him and accepted the divine shield and sword while Iolaos stared with eyes wide.

A moment later, without saying a word, Hermes ascended, not as a star but as an eagle.

I prayed my thanks to the gods, and then Iolaos and I sat down by the light of a torch to admire these divinely handcrafted items of warfare. They were forged, I learned later, by wondrous Hephaestos, the god of fire. On the shield were inscribed scenes of the origins of the gods—how Earth gave birth to Sky, and how they mated to produce Mountains and Ocean. In the beautifully etched scenes we seemed to witness how Zeus, son of Rhea and wicked Cronos, had led Cronos' children in their fight against their father, and how my father had seized power, splitting the dominion of the universe into three, with his brother Hades ruling the underworld, Poseidon the sea, and himself the heavens. The whole story flashed into our eyes from the brilliant shield. But then our eyes were taken with the sword: the hilt was studded with gems, and enameled pictures showed the birth of great Athene, who entered life from the brow of Zeus; and on the reverse side Hephaestos had depicted the birth of the bewitching goddess of love, his wife Aphrodite, from the sea foam.

I remarked to Iolaos, "Remember your encounter with Hermes, lad, for the appearance of a god on earth—undisguised, plain to see—is very rare." With that, I bid him goodnight, and told him that I would visit him again after I returned from Lerna.

He scowled and would not look at me; he was disappointed that after all I would not rescue him from his disagreeable guardian. Meanwhile, I lay down content, and slept well, full of confidence that my venture into Lerna was blessed by the gods and destined for success.

I set out before dawn, before anyone was awake. I noticed but did not think anything of a bundle on the floorboard of the chariot; I assumed that it was a gift from a well-wisher. As morning light poured over my horses and me, however, I heard a groan at my feet.

Then I saw a rustling within the bundle. I laughed and said with a sigh, "Oh, how I wish Iolaos were here to accompany me!"

"Uncle Hercules!" came a voice, and then out popped Iolaos' head from the bundle. "Here I am!"

We were too far along for me to return him home, and, besides, I liked the boy's pluck, only wishing that I at his age had had an uncle going off on dangerous expeditions.

"Stand up beside me, Iolaos, and take charge of the horses!"

I sat on the floor in his place and let him drive the horses over the curving roads from Tiryns. We would have a long journey, and the sooner he gained confidence of his control over the chariot the better. I hummed to myself and looked off in a casual way to the left and right, pretending I was easy about every turn he made. That night we slept under the stars.

In the morning we started early and arrived in Lerna before noon. There, by the shores of the bottomless Alcyonian Lake, we followed the path of destruction through the swamplands toward the nine-headed hydra's lair. We had to leave the chariot on a dry mound overlooking the lake because the swamp would have sucked down our wheels, and the lake's monsters would have swallowed our horses alive. Iolaos, reckless boy, followed at my heels as I cut through the tangled vines and called out a challenge to that snaky offspring of hideous monsters: "Hydra! Come on out and meet your fate! Your death has arrived in Hercules!"

"And I, Iolaos, shall help him!" he cried out.

"Shh!" I commanded.

"Shhh!" I heard in return. "SHHHHH!"

For a moment I thought the boy was mocking me! But then we heard it—HISSSS!

We saw nothing but the trees and the swampy water at our feet. When Iolaos caught up to me, I took his arm and said, "Stay here until I call for you." There was a darkness in my tone that prevented the boy from questioning me.

"Yesss," he whispered.

I crept onward as alert as any deer that has heard the footsteps of a lion. Nothing could keep my sandals, however, from their muddy smacking. By the time I reached the flats near the hydra's lair, its nine heads were hissing a dangerous welcome. The snaky monster's body was the size of a tree trunk. Eight of its heads branched off in different directions, while the one in the middle, with sparkling eyes of frosty blue, spat sparks of fire. Never for a moment did I lose my courage, but for the first and last time during my labors I understood faintheartedness.

However, as soon as it raised its necks to strike, I leapt forward with my sword to strike first.

What enemy has ever doubled its dangerousness with every blow it receives? Only the hydra, that monster! In the few heartbeats that passed after each chop of my sword, wherein I sliced off all but the head in the

As soon as the hydra raised its necks to strike,
I leapt forward with my sword to strike first.

middle, two heads sprang to life on each stump. I could
scarcely believe my eyes. Foolishly I swung my sword
again and the sixteen new heads flew off—but only
heartbeats later they became thirty-two. I am a vain
man! What did I do next but swing at those snapping,
hissing snake heads and create sixty-four!

The one in the middle—the one I later discovered to
be immortal—now hissed a stream of fire, which I
blocked with Hephaestos' shield. The flames bounced
away, but caused several branches surrounding us to
catch fire. The hydra recoiled for just one moment, and
in that instant Athene herself seemed to speak to me;
suddenly wisdom filled my mind, and I called out
for Iolaos.

Fine boy, he had already crept very close, and was
presently at my side, beaming with happiness during
one of the most desperate times of my life! I backed
away for a moment from the hydra's poisonous heads
and picked off a burning branch from the tree above
me. A tremendous crab then crawled over from the
swamp to lend assistance to its snake-headed comrade.
The crab pinched my sandaled right foot, and I bel-
lowed out in pain.

"Quick!" I called out. "Listen, Iolaos—yow! (the crab
pinched me harder)—take the torch—yow!" I paused a
moment in my battle with the hydra to give the crab a
swift kick; the creature flew, claws and legs akimbo,
through the trees and back into the swamp.

I shook my pinched foot to restore feeling to it and
said to Iolaos, handing him the fiery branch, "Take this,
and the moment I slice off one of this monster's heads,
seal the neck with the fire. It's the flowing blood,
I believe, that creates two heads for one." Just then the
monster struck for us and the immortal head spit
its fire.

"Quick! Be ready!" I shouted. When the fire from its mouth ceased for a moment, we ran at the hydra, my shield protecting us, and then I swung the sword, clipping off two or three snaky heads at a time. With each strike Iolaos touched the fire to the necks and sealed the blood within. Now that the monster did not redouble its poisonousness I was able to overcome it.

It was the immortal blue-eyed head that I had to deal with alone. When I had sliced the head from its body, I took a leather cord from my sandal and muzzled that fiery mouth. Iolaos provided me with his leather sack, into which I threw the hydra's head, a head no bigger than a crocodile's.

The snaky trunk of the body we cut up and cooked till the poison began to flow. Then we collected the poison in a jar, for use on my arrows. Perhaps it would have been better for me had we not done this, for this poison eventually took away my mortal life.

At the time, however, Iolaos and I were giddy with our success. We returned through the mucky swamp to the chariot. We hunted, caught some game, cooked and ate. I was as cheerful and happy as the boy. We celebrated, gave thanks to the gods for their aid and called ourselves heroes.

On the chariot drive back to Tiryns I told Iolaos that for a time, perhaps a year, I would have to do without his help, and that in the meantime he should continue his education in the art of archery and swordsmanship.

He was crestfallen, but he did not squawk or make a fuss. After all, he had helped the great Hercules defeat a deadly menace.

When we appeared before Eurystheus, however, and I told of my victory over the hydra and showed him the head, the cunning king said, "Your story surprises me. When I asked you to defeat the hydra, I meant you and no one else! You get no credit for that labor, none at all!"

"There was no rule against a boy aiding me——"

"There is a rule now," said Eurystheus. "And that labor does not count!"

I had gained nothing by killing the hydra but poison for my arrows!

The king laughed, taunting me, and I wanted to kill him, but Athene came and gripped me by the back of my hair, yanking very hard to get my attention, and told me to nod and obey.

I nodded.

"Very well," said Eurystheus. "Now bring me the golden horns of the Cerynean hind."

"That deer belongs to the goddess Artemis," I reminded him. "What is a god's is not for men. If I killed such a deer the goddess would certainly kill me."

"You refuse, then?"

"No," I said, desperately trying to think of a solution to this dilemma. To myself I said, "I shall not kill that deer. But what am I to do, since unless that deer is dead it will not give up its golden horns."

After I buried the hydra's immortal head under a rock on the road to Lerna, I left for Artemis' forest, which was not very far away. In two or three days I arrived in the valley of Argolis. I erected an altar dedicated to Artemis, the goddess of hunting, and I prayed to her. Where would I be without the friendship and wisdom of Athene? She came to me as if in a dream, and spoke these words: "Think, Hercules, think: did Eurystheus demand that you *kill* the deer?"

"No!" I replied. "But how do I bring him the horns without harming the deer?"

"Do not harm the deer," replied Athene, seeming to answer from within my own mind. "Bring to Eurystheus the deer, unharmed, horns and all. If he wishes to murder the deer for its horns, let him do so and let him suffer Artemis' revenge."

"Yes!" I answered. "But this deer will not allow me to capture it without a fight, will it?"

"A weary opponent will give himself up to you."

Weary! How long did I track Artemis' deer? Almost a year. It was an unhappy and long pursuit. At the end of that year I was so weary I would have given myself up

I picked him up, threw him over my shoulders,
and started off on my hike back to Tiryns.

to the deer had he wanted me to. But Athene was right. After those months of chasing him up mountains and through rivers and streams, he finally lay down in front of me, tired of running away.

"I will not harm you," I reassured the gorgeous stag. As with so many beasts before and after, I picked him up and threw him over my shoulders, gripping his slender, hard-hoofed feet in my right hand, my knobby club in my left, and I started off on my hike back to Tiryns.

I released the deer the moment we came within the palace doors. "Here," I told Eurystheus, "I have brought you the golden horns you so desired."

"The hind is alive!"

"You have a sharp eye!" I laughed. "But remember, you asked for the horns. So I have brought them to you. It's now up to you to do what you want about the deer to which they are attached!" I laughed again.

He was furious with me, but no fool. He commanded the priests from Artemis' temple to come and take the deer back to Artemis' forest. Had he killed the hind, Artemis in her rage would have hunted him down and killed him and everyone he loved.

Eurystheus sulked and pouted, and spent the rest of the day thinking of another task. He called me to appear before him and said, "For once and for the last time you have outwitted me, Hercules. Your next labor is to capture the Erymanthian boar, that demonish destroyer of the countryside in Arcadia!"

For a moment I thought he was giving me a tiresome but easy task, but then he laughed in a mocking spirit and said, "Because you tricked me with the hind, I punish you with a demand of my own. When I say 'capture,' I mean 'capture alive'!"

"Alive!" I said, outraged at his spiteful request. For as you might know, a boar is easier killed than captured alive, fiercesome wild pig that it is. Think of Odysseus, that hero from Ithaca who followed my generation. As a young lad a long-tusked boar gashed him through the thigh, as no warrior was ever able to do. And those who had seen it said the boar in Arcadia was twice the size of the largest boar ever known, and ten times as destructive and mean.

5. The Centaurs and the Boar

MY FIRST day on the road I came upon the tracks of a horse and decided to follow them for a distance. Which of us does not have an animal nature? I, for one, think of myself as somewhat lionish, what with my kingly presence, my great bulk, my savagery in fighting and my huge voice. However, even garbed in my lion's robe, I do not resemble very closely a flesh and blood lion.

But do you know of those men who stand upon the four legs of a horse? Where a horse's neck would be is the trunk of a man's body, from belly to arms and hands. His head and face is wild with beard and curls, but all man. His horsiness consists of his four legs and that horsy body. These strange man-horses are known as centaurs. They are mortal but their mother, Nephele, was a cloud, which perhaps accounts for their changeable nature. They are a wise but wild bunch, and Cheiron, great Cheiron, the best of centaurs, was the teacher of such heroes as Achilles and my future comrade Jason. I hesitate to say—oh, shameful admission!—that I took Cheiron's life.

I must tell a short tale now that does me little credit. A hero's life, I remind you, contains not only his noble and brave actions but also his follies and errors.

That trail of hooves I was following belonged to the centaur Pholos. He was hunting wild game, not needing a bow and arrow, as I might, but only a spear. I came to a rocky ridge overlooking a valley and watched as what looked like a man on horseback gave chase to a fleet, proud ram. The ram's horns curled in several wide, thick loops, ending in sharpened points. But for all its nimbleness among the rocky steeps, the ram could not elude the masterful hunter's spear.

Having thrown the ram over his horsy back, the centaur came up the valley to see who I was. He had some doubt about me, being that I was "one of those rickety-legged creatures"—that is, a man.

"What do you want?" he called out.

"Nothing, friend. I was admiring your sure-footed hunting."

He smiled at the compliment and at a distance of thirty or forty yards introduced himself. "I am Pholos, one of the race of centaurs. If you care to join me for supper, please follow me."

He loped away, through dense forest, challenging me to keep up. It was not long before we came to a mountainside wall of rough boulders. He moved one aside, revealing a cave, and beckoned me within. "Welcome, Hercules!" Pholos said. "Yes, I know your name, for who else among the rickety-legged could possibly keep up with a centaur?"

His cave was lit and warmed by a large fire. A hole in the cave-top drew up the smoke, keeping the cave well-aired. When I sat upon my haunches near Pholos, next to the fire, he offered me a piece of the ram's meat. I was surprised that he had not bothered to cook it, even for a moment.

Seeing my surprise, he said, "We like our meat raw," and sighed with pleasure just before he stuffed a piece of bloody flesh into his toothy, grinning mouth.

I picked up a long stick, sharpened it with my sword, and then fastened the meat upon it. As my appetite began to grow, Pholos offered me a cup of wine, which I drank off in an instant. Then, his mouth still hardily chewing raw ram, he seemed to panic as he said, "Oh, oh, dear me, Hercules, we are out of wine, and I have no more to offer you or to drink myself."

But I, now to my regret, spied a barrel in the high reaches of his rocky cave. "What about that, what's in there?" I asked. To point out drink that a host does not offer is bad manners, yet I did so.

"Oh, no," he stammered. "That is sacred wine, to be opened only upon a solemn occasion and offered to the gods. Besides, it is too strong for mortals like ourselves."

"Nonsense!" I said. I was a young man, sure of my strength to resist potent drink. "Let's have it!"

I had put him in an awkward position. Was it preferable to deny a guest, or to risk the effects of sacred wine? Pholos, good-hearted, weak-willed centaur, gave in to my insistent requests. I was without mercy for his qualms.

"What are we?" I said. "Children of immortal beings! Your mother a cloud, my father the god of gods. If we cannot drink it without fear of catastrophe, who can?"

Pholos weakened. "Just a half cup each, how about that? As I said, it's supposed to be very strong. We'll weaken it by adding three or four parts water."

"Agreed," I said.

Pholos clambered up the cave walls. The cave entrance was sealed by a boulder, but, as I told you, there was a hole at the top of the cave so the smoke could escape. We forgot this in our lust for the wine. We admired ourselves for limiting the outpouring of the fragrant wine to one cup before we sealed and returned the barrel to its hiding place.

"Fragrant"? Have you walked through a meadow of flowers on a warm, still spring day? Its fragrance is thicker than air, sweeter than honey. This wine, even in our mixture of it in a bucket of water, sent delicious fumes into our heads and into the air and out the smoke-hole. Within moments, as bees are drawn to flowers, Pholos' brother centaurs swarmed to the cave, some on top near the hole, others outside the bouldered entrance.

"Pholos!" they yelled. "Let us in! Let us have some of that wine!"

Pholos' brother centaurs swarmed to the cave, and yelled, "Let us have some of that wine!"

They burst through the hole atop the ceiling, falling to the floor of the cave. They pushed and moved aside the boulder and came in that way as well. There were a dozen, the youngest and rowdiest of the high-spirited centaurs, filled with desire for the wine. "Let us have it!" they cried.

Had we not already opened the barrel, they would not have found the wine, but the fragrance turned them into bloodhounds, and with no trouble they scrambled up the rocks and began their unwatered-down drinking. They became crazed, quarrelsome, and as soon as the wine was polished off, and the empty barrel came crashing onto the floor, a riot broke out. Pholos and I found ourselves attacked, accused of holding out on further supplies of wine.

We denied it, but try arguing with a gang of drunken centaurs! Pholos and I attempted to leave the cave and let them fight among themselves. Instead they encircled us as if we were their enemy, so I warned them. "Step back and let us pass. Continue, if you like, with your drunken party, but let us go in peace."

At that Pholos was struck by two of his brothers, and I was shoved by another. I pushed them away, pulled Pholos to me and gave us cover behind the boulder while I strung my bow. The centaurs thought they were invulnerable to my death-dealing arrows. I shot one, I shot another, and still they rushed at us.

Cheiron, the great noble centaur, teacher of heroes, came to the cave, having heard our battle, and called out, "Let this fighting stop!"

His brother, Xenop, drunkenly rushed at him, and so I shot my never-erring bow. The arrow clipped Xenop through the throat, a fine shot, except that it continued and found a second mark—Cheiron's thigh.

Cheiron fell, and as I fought off the rowdy centaurs, I made my way to him. But what mortal can resist the death that lives in the hydra's poison? Cheiron, a master healer, instructed me and Pholos to mix various leaves and herbs and apply them to his wound. "Death will come," he said, "but not with such agony as the hydra's poison gives."

On seeing the fate of Cheiron, the other centaurs fled, and so Pholos and I were able to make the numbing medicine. Poor Cheiron! Wretched Hercules! Had I not demanded the wine, this death would not have happened. I cursed myself and prayed to Hermes, deliverer of souls, to make Cheiron's journey into Hades an easy one.

I erected an altar to Hermes and then bade farewell to unhappy Pholos. I then began my overdue labor.

Not once but dozens of times over the course of the next year, as I tracked the boar through forests, across ravines and rivers and into the mountains, he turned and faced me, his pursuer, his throaty voice squealing. He had slobberingly whetted his tusks till they were sharp as spears. He would charge me, surprised when I set down my weapons and dodged his thrusts. For I could not kill him or I would violate the rules set down by Eurystheus. But such a beast could not be harnessed or roped. No, only my bare hands could possibly take him alive and hold him.

Shall I tell you of the long weary nights and the hot, slow days wherein I tracked the boar? No, for that would be no gift, but a chore, a labor on your mind as it was on my body. My only recreation was eating. Never did I have so much time in my life for hunting. Athene, divine, wise goddess, would come to me on occasion, disguised always as a young boy or old woman, pretending to have been searching the woods on Mount Erymanthos for nuts.

"Hello," she would say, a basket in hand.

She always fooled me, at first, and I would say, "Beware, young man (or old woman), the terrible boar has just passed by. You are in danger of its dreadful spear-like tusks."

And the child (or old woman), eyes shining in that owlish way of Athene's, would laugh, and reply, "Have no fear for me, hero. I come from Olympos, home of the gods, to watch your progress."

"Athene!" I would say.

Laughing, then twittering like the bird she suddenly became, she would fly away.

*A look of fear—the first and last time,
I am sure—crossed the boar's face.*

Such visits gave me the will to go on.

It was nearly a year before I had pressed the boar to exhaustion. Still, had not Zeus, my father, delivered a snowstorm over the peaks of Mount Erymanthos, the boar might have eluded me for months more. The snow

fell in beautiful flakes, creating a soft world of white-
ness, a blanket of powder higher than the boar's glis-
tening tusks. Whenever he tried to run he sank. I easily
followed his track. He was as tired as I, yet blindly
pushed on. At last I saw my chance to get my hands
on him.

A look of fear—the first and last time, I am sure—
crossed that animal's face. He made a show of turning,
snorting, but he had no intention of trying to charge. He
could not. The snow made his movements slow and
awkward.

I continued in his track and then made my move.
Have you seen a bird dive for the surface of a lake,
where it clips up into its mouth a long, flopping fish? I
charged at the boar and then dove under his belly, and
rose as quick as a bird, the boar not in my mouth but
atop my shoulders, my hands cupping his feet together
in front of my chest. The boar snorted—what an absurd
picture he made! A fearsome killer riding atop a man's
shoulders like any gentle deer or child!

He snorted all the two-day-long journey back to
Eurystheus' palace, during which journey I met a handsome boy named Hylas, the princely son of King
Theiodamas. He told me about the expedition in quest
of the Golden Fleece that noble Jason was planning.
Hylas was eager to join, though he was hardly fifteen
years old. I could not bear the thought of missing out
on adventures to distant lands with other young
heroes, and so when I returned to Tiryns, I left the boar
tied to the gate of the king's throne room and told a
guard to tell Eurystheus I would be back in a year to
complete my labors.

6. I Clean the Augean Stables

JASON WAS the son of Aeson and the grandson of Aeolos, the lord of the island of Aeolia and Zeus's keeper of the winds. Jason needed to set sail to the distant Black Sea to kill the dreaded dragon that guarded the Golden Fleece. The possession of this fleece would restore his father's kingdom to him.

When Hylas and I arrived at the port in Thessaly, however, Jason accepted us but was not as pleased to recruit us as I had expected. Being that I was already famed for my strength and courage, and he was comparatively unknown, he feared that his assembled heroes would elect me as their captain.

When the vote came, it went as he expected. Jason, that luckless man, who lived to regret his life, conceded the captaincy to me, but I refused the honor.

"This quest is Jason's!" I declared, "and so he shall lead us."

My decision was for the best, as I abandoned the voyage when tragedy claimed my dear friend Hylas.

I will not describe the amazing ship, the *Argo*, which sailed as if by magic, or the monsters we battled after our passage through the Hellespont, that narrow strait between Asia and Europe. Instead, I shall speak of when we lost the wind for a time and had to rely on our oars. "I did not know my own strength" is a common expression, and that is just what I said when I snapped my oar in two in the blue-green waters. My comrades suggested we pull ashore to a wooded land beside a river on the Asian side of the Sea of Marmara.

While our shipmates made camp, Hylas and I wandered into the woods, he to find water, I to find the best tree to make into an oar.

As fond as I was of Iolaos, who was nearly a nephew of mine, I was just as fond of Hylas. I must now relate the details of his death, a task which seems beyond any Eurystheus assigned me.

What happiness he and I might have shared on the voyage of the Argonauts! How proud we were to be helping Jason. But tragedy came when I least expected it. He had gone up the river canyon, carrying jugs and pitchers, to fetch the purest fresh water. He leaned over a sweet-smelling spring and a nymph, those divine women who live in the waters and woods and thereby give them the spirit of life, was so attracted to his beauty that she reached out from the waters and pulled him in.

I did not see this and I only learned the details much later when I entered Olympos as an immortal. No, at the time Hylas was made the bridegroom of the spring's nymph, I was busily uprooting a massive tree to make into my oar. I do remember hearing a surprising splash. I looked up and called out, "Hylas!"

There was no answer.

I walked along the canyon where I knew he had gone and saw no sign of him but saw his jugs and pitchers on the grassy bank beside the spring. Have you ever seen a lost hound searching for his master? He is frantic, sniffing everywhere, not finding any clue. Just so was I, running through the woods, calling to my shipmates, who, less fearful than I, less concerned, tried to reassure me. "He's followed another trail to another spring. He'll be back," said Jason.

The fool! Hylas never came back. I passed by the spring a dozen times, I peered into its depths, and I lowered myself into its icy waters. But the nymph knew the value of the boy she had stolen and did not let me detect him.

I refused to leave, even the next day, when Jason ordered the men back on the ship. "Without Hylas, I can sail no more," I told him.

"So be it," he said. "The wind has come back to us. We must sail."

I bade him farewell. Some say that Zeus, watchful father, did not want me to dally away from my labors any longer, and that he thereby encouraged the nymph in her kidnapping of Hylas. But Zeus tells me no, that he was content to let me continue with Jason's voyage, and that the true story is that Hylas was stolen because of his beauty.

In any case, I returned with sadness to Eurystheus, who, it turned out, resented my long absence and had come up with a labor with which he meant to shame me.

"I command you——" Eurystheus said, before laughing so hard he could not speak another word for several moments. He took up a piece of his kingly robe and wiped his eyes before he was able to go on. "Go to King Augeas, he of the famous cattle yards . . . and, in a single day, clear out the dung from his stables! That is your labor, Hercules!"

I, Hercules, cart away tons of manure! In one day? Had I known ahead of time the immensity of the heaps of dung I might have retired from the labors then and there. But, after all, what labor not of one's will is ever a complete pleasure?

Augeas was the king of Elis, that northwestern region of the Peloponnese, and though he was rich on account of his herds of cattle, he had allowed their stables to fill so high with manure they had become impassable and unusable.

I did not inform Augeas that I came to his land to fulfill a task for Eurystheus. Instead I held my nose and told him, "Allow me, wealthy king, to clean out your stables today."

"Help yourself," said Augeas. "Zeus knows I couldn't do it in a year! I'll grant you a tenth of my herds should you succeed."

"One tenth of all your wealth!" I said.

"That's about right," he said. "And good luck. Now over there you'll find a shovel."

I dragged my feet to the hut where he had pointed, and looked with helplessness on such a tool. I leaned on the shovel and gazed out at the lovely view of the countryside and beyond to the Menius River, a blue ribbon winding past Elis.

"If I should somehow succeed in shoveling this manure away, I will bathe for hours in those cleansing waters!" I remarked to myself.

For once it was not Athene who supplied me with a good idea—I inspired myself. Tossing away the shovel, I rushed back into the hut, where I found halters for yoking cattle. I picked out the four largest bovine beasts and arranged them in a team, with me standing atop the widest plow I could find, and a sharp-edged boulder in addition dragging behind. We would cut a channel to the river.

"Onward!" I cried, and snapped the reins. The cattle, only too happy to be driven out of the messy stableyard, pulled me along. The channel was no wider than a creekbed, but it was well-shaped and deep. In the afternoon we reached the river, and in the next phase of the sun after that, with only a short while to go until sundown and failure, I set about damming the river to divert its flow into my empty creekbed.

Other men may be more clever than I, but this was one time I was justly proud of my wisdom. The dammed river found my creekbed and then raced along it, faster almost than I could run alongside. In little time it arrived at the stableyards, where, with that lonesome shovel, I directed the stream in the directions it was most needed. The water washed through the stables and the yard, collecting the manure with it, and then coursed down out of the yard and into a low pocket of wooded land between the pasturelands, where it formed a somewhat muddy and smelly lake.

When the yard was cleaner than it had been since creation, I hurried back to the spot where I had dammed the river and broke it free once again, giving thanks to the guardian nymph of its crystal waters. I shored up the creek and drove Augeas' fine cattle back to the stables.

For once I was the hero of animals instead of their hunter. Augeas, on the other hand, turned pale when he returned that evening and saw the tremendous feat I had performed.

"I believe you said one-tenth of your cattle, king," I reminded him.

Was I wrong to expect payment when it had been promised to me? Though Eurystheus would soon hold me blameworthy, I hope you do not. For what man offered a prize without having asked for it does not begin to dream of that prize as expectantly as a man who has demanded it?

But Augeas was a cheat and said, "I never would have offered you such a stake of my cattle had I thought you capable of cleaning the stables in a day! You deceived me into thinking it impossible!"

"I did not trick you, king, by words or action."

"I cannot pay you what you ask," he countered. "Please, instead, accept with my warmest appreciation . . . you walked here, didn't you, from Tiryns?"

"Yes."

"Then, I grant you . . . " At this moment we heard a braying from the barn, and Augeas smiled and said, " . . . my trusty, humble yet dependable mule, Rocky."

I was angry, but what could I do? I had many more labors to perform and killing Augeas was not part of the labor Eurystheus required of me. I took the mule, poor broken down work-animal, but after a dozen yards I had to give up riding it, it moaned so. It could not take my pack or weapons as a load either, so I carried those and let him follow in my tracks.

Eurystheus was amused at the image I presented when I arrived at his court.

"Do you return with a donkey because you have failed and are ashamed, Hercules?" he asked.

"No," I replied, "I succeeded, as usual. This donkey was the payment I received from Augeas for my amazing feat of cleaning his stables."

Cunning Eurystheus smiled with an unbecoming humor and said, "Dear me, Hercules. You have accepted payment for a task I assigned you. That can hardly count as a labor, then. Just as with the hydra, you have not satisfied the terms of our contract. You still owe me seven more labors. But, believe me, you shall not live through them all! For your next task, go chase away the Stymphalian birds. You'll have your hands full with them, I tell you!"

I choked off my hot anger at his cheating ways and departed.

7. The Birds and the Bull

I ARRIVED SEVERAL days later at Lake Stymphalos. The birds had made themselves a menace by flocking in enormous numbers, arranging themselves so densely on the edges of the lake that no men from the neighboring city could fish or could even protect themselves should the birds attack. These tall, leggy birds had long, sharp beaks that could stab a man through his chest and claws that could pierce his limbs. Even with a bow and arrows there were too many thousands for me to kill. While I was surveying this strange scene from a hilltop, good, wise Athene, disguised as a boy, fishing pole over his shoulder, a cap on his head, came and sat down at my left, and said, "My father says thunder, though it causes no harm, is the most frightful weapon of all."

"The most frightful weapon?" I said, wondering what riddle the boy was posing to me.

He handed me a pair of bronze castanets. And then I understood! "Thank you, lad," I said, offering him my hand. "So handsome are you, so gleaming are your eyes I feel you must be a divine god or goddess."

The boy turned his head away, smiling, and then in the form of an owl flew off toward the heavens. Owlish Athene!

I hiked down the hilltop, pulled my shield close over me to prevent the birds' sharp beaks from piercing me, and then waded into the shallows of the lake. Like a dancer at a feast, I clicked those castanets. What a clanging din I raised! A stony silence, however, followed the first few thunderous knocks—a moment later, as I again clicked the castanets in rhythm, the birds screeched in fright and flapped their wings hastily and flew in droves up and away. So many were there that they shut out the sunlight for several minutes. I roared with laughter all the while, but kept up the terrible brass din until they were all gone.

I prayed thankfulness to Athene and then returned to Tiryns.

"What cannot you do?" wondered Eurystheus. For once he seemed not my enemy but almost my admirer, marvelling at my strength and cleverness.

"I do not know," I replied, "since I have never failed."

"I'll see what I can do about that," he said. He thought for several minutes and then said, "Perhaps your saving grace is that these previous labors have kept you in the friendly confines of the Peloponnesian peninsula. Go and bring me the savage Cretan bull alive. You might already know, Hercules, that his monstrous offspring, the Minotaur, half-bull, half-human, ate up all who visited its pen within the winding, confusing labyrinth."

"You shall have the Cretan bull to do with as you will," I answered. I fetched dear Iolaos, who was now a hearty young man, and with him sailed across the sea to the vast island of Crete.

This bull had mated with Pasiphae, wife of King Minos, producing the Minotaur, a creature more stubborn than any bull and more fiercesome than any man. The father bull now spent his days wandering the hills above the city, and then rushing down into the fields of farmers, goring their cattle and destroying with powerful kicks their lovely walled fields.

I expected the aid of Minos, considering this bull was hardly his friend or the friend of his people, but when

Iolaos and I appeared at his court, Minos glared at us, stroking his bearded chin, and seemed to begrudge us even a piece of bread or cup of water.

"We shall capture the bull, with your permission," I said.

"My permission?" he said. "Kill him, dance with him, I don't care what you do with him. I do not think of him, and I will lend you no help. I washed my hands of that beast many years ago."

Angry at his words, I thought about challenging him to fight. But Iolaos, acting as my Athene, whispered that we neither needed nor desired Minos' aid, and that to fight him would only bring down on us the splendid armies of Crete.

We stalked out of the palace and began our plan. We would carry no weapons but my club, to keep us from accidentally killing the savage beast. We climbed a mountain trail to the bull's usual pasturage and passed a crude signboard depicting a fire-breathing, bloody-horned bull. I told Iolaos to wait by the sign and that I would return shortly.

To my surprise the bull was asleep at the top of the trail, but at first I mistook it for a tremendous black boulder. Then, recognizing it for what it was, instead of turning and running as most men would do, or sneaking up on it and lassoing its feet, as only the bravest men would think of doing, I walked up to the heaving, sighing, dozing bull and grabbed it by its fly-swishing tail.

The bull leaped as if it had been stung. But buck as it would, it could not shake me away. He bucked for the good part of an afternoon, until the sweat poured off him in streams. Finally, however, he was humbled, and the Cretan bull followed me and Iolaos down the mountainside, through the city, where we jeered at Minos

The Cretan bull bucked until the sweat poured off him in streams.

watching us from his palace, and then finally climbed aboard our ship. With gentle winds, we sailed for Tiryns.

The Cretan bull was twice the size of the largest bull anyone had ever seen. When we led it into the courtyard of Eurystheus' palace, the king screamed in fright.

"Are you satisfied?" I asked.

"No! Get it out of here!" said Eurystheus.

I bowed and released the bull. He bucked and stormed, kicking over pedestals and statues within the palace before running crazily through the countryside.

Eurystheus was angry and for my next labor sent me on my longest quest so far, to distant Thrace for King Diomedes' mares, horses about whose nature I knew nothing.

8. I Wrestle with Death and Meet the Man-eating Horses

I WAS far along in the routine of my labors. Sure of myself and of the successful outcome of my tasks, I told Iolaos to stay at home while I went on the long road to Thrace, in northern Greece.

While crossing Thessaly, I decided to visit Admetus, king of Pherae, in eastern Thessaly. Admetus, a fine sailor, was a friend I had made on my short journey with the Argonauts. When I came to the trail entrance that would take me down into the valley where Admetus' palace lay, a stocky, wide-shouldered marauder, cloaked and holding a spear, leapt down from a boulder before me.

"Hand over your possessions, traveler," he said, threatening to poke the spear at me.

I laughed! What did he take me for, chopped oats?

"Don't laugh!" he shrieked. "What makes you too tough for my sharp spear?"

"Tell me your name, bold robber. Then, when I have finished laughing, I will kill you and keep your name alive in my memory, a fool for my tales."

"I didn't catch but a bit of that," said the slow-witted man, "but, all right, they call me One-armed Burly."

Out from his cloak came his right arm cut off at the elbow.

Seeing my glance, he said quickly, "I had an accident."

"You're about to have another," I said.

"I was left-handed to begin with! My right arm was only in the way. Now don't stare, and tell me your name and then prepare to meet your fallen friends in Hades."

"Very well, Burly. My name is Hercules, and my father is Zeus."

In confusion Burly dropped his spear. "Even so!" he cried, his voice quivering, "I'll kill you and live for ever as the man who slayed mighty, mighty, mighty Hercules."

"Give up your robbing, and make way, or your life's soon complete."

This daredevil thought about that; I could almost hear the stones tumble in his head. Then he answered, "Should I kill you, I'd own your fine cloak of lion skin, your gleaming shield so beautifully worked I am hardly able to look away from it. Your bow is taller than I am; in itself it must be worth a king's riches." He picked up his spear and poised it, but his gaze was taking in my form, for I had stood up from my fit of laughing.

He was terrified. My muscles shone with the warmth of my body. Just as a small animal is fixed in place by the eyes of a snake, so Burly fell into my gaze.

He shook his head to clear the spell and cried out, "Give—give—give up your shield, Hercules, and I'll not kill-kill you."

Terrified by his own threat, he launched his spear. Puny little man, his spear missed by several feet to the left. He cowered, awaiting, it seemed, the fatal blow from my sword or shot from my bow. Instead I stamped my foot at him, and he fell over, backward, into the dust. He got up and ran down the trail, screaming, "Help! Help!"

Fool! The citizens of Pherae, recognizing him for the robber who had been harassing them, caught him and soon put him on trial for his crimes.

When I reached the palace, however, there was a strange quiet, and the guards at the city walls hung their heads as I approached, hardly seeming to care, it seemed, whether I were friend or foe. I, on the other hand, was giddy with my good fortune, my recent successes with the labors and, finally, with the thought of seeing my friend Admetus.

I entered the hall where I expected we would share many feasts. A sullen servant went to announce my arrival to him. After a long wait, which was not flattering to me, his friend and the hero of great fame, Admetus entered the hall and, with head lowered, greeted me, saying, "Hercules, dearest friend, welcome."

"Admetus!" I answered. "Why so gloomy?"

"I do not wish to spoil your visit with my troubles," he said. "Let us talk of something else."

But the gloom was a dark cloud over his head, and there was no pleasure in talk.

"Tell me," I finally asked, "are your noble parents dead or alive?"

"Alive!" he said.

"Then why so downcast? Is it a relative of yours that has left this world?"

He said, after a moment, "No, certainly not a relative, but Death has come for someone else."

"Death comes for us all!" I said, shaking him by the shoulder. "As you know, I am not a philosophical or ponderous man, yet I try to be sensible, and I do not like needless mournfulness. So come now, if it's not a relative, then how does it affect us? I've been so eager to see you, my dear friend, but now I am here, you seem hardly fit for company or joyous feasting."

"I am not, indeed, fit for company or feasting, dear Hercules."

I became angry. Alas, why did Zeus bless me with his heavy-browed temper? I reasoned that since no relative of his had died, that the mourning was for show.

"I am your guest!" I shouted. "And I demand the service any guest, least of all a friend and hero, deserves—I want a feast!" I thought I could provoke him into a return to our old ways.

Admetus, scarcely able to speak, said, "As you wish."

He ordered a feast, but I have never shared such a dull table. He was not interested in hearing of my great deeds, nor in my adventures. He did not laugh when I told him of Burly, the one-armed bandit. When I finished my drinking and eating, I rose and told him that he had made it plain he no longer considered me a friend.

"You are my friend, and that is why I spare you my pain," he replied.

I left the hall and decided to go on to Thrace, to my labor of capturing Diomedes' horses. As I stood at the city's gates, disgusted with Admetus and his treatment of me, shouting out, in fact, my bitter disappointment in the king's poor reception, I overheard a brave guard mutter, "It's a wretch who curses his mourning friend."

"What's that you say!" I thundered. I ran up to the guard, and he leaned away in dread. He did not answer, so I said, "Admetus grieves no relative! Why should he mourn!"

"So would you mourn in the evening, cold Hercules, if your wife was led away by Death in the morning."

"Wife!" I was struck by the word. "Wife! But Admetus never told me of his marriage! How did she die? Who is she?" Yes, a wife is not a relative by blood, but there is a bond of love between them, stronger than blood, bonds forged by the fire god Hephaestos at the request of his wife, goddess of love Aphrodite. I struck myself on the head, nearly knocking myself out. The guard was now too frightened of me to speak. I shook him. "Tell me what happened!"

"Alcestis—whom he wed on his journey with Jason—is his wife —the most noble, good wife who ever lived! And she lived until today—when Death came for her husband. God Apollo protects Admetus in return for an earlier favor, and came to a bargain with Death that would allow someone else to take the king's place. Alcestis' love was so great for her husband that she offered herself as Admetus' substitute. Death saw gold where he would have taken silver and gladly accepted Alcestis' offer."

I cursed myself, turning my terrible temper on myself. But Athene, it must have been—because who gives us wisdom when we seem at our wits' end?— whispered in my ear, "If you've wrestled the Nemean lion, you can wrestle Death."

"Quick," I said to the guard, "where is the queen's tomb?"

"Yonder," he said, pointing to a grove nearby.

I ran off in that direction. It was evening. I found Alcestis' tomb; it was within the future tomb of Admetus, and on its threshold lay an offering to Death of food and flowers. I sampled a pinch of the food and spat it out—too salty for anyone but Death! In any event, he had not passed this way, and I still had a chance to fight him. I crept behind the tomb and waited. It was night before he came, but the moon was out and bright.

He was cloaked, as grim Death should be, hidden from mortal eyes, but beside him walked a beautiful, dark-haired maiden; her gaze through her funeral veil was calm, proud, almost happy that she had sacrificed herself for her husband. Though Admetus was my friend, I confessed to myself that she was too good for him, that he should not have allowed her to be taken by Death in his place.

Just as Death stooped to take a bite of his salty dish, I leapt out, grasped his strong arms and pulled them behind his back. "Let her go!" I spoke into his ear, keeping my eyes from his depthless face.

He struggled, and I could see the confusion in his movements—wondering what beast in human form could have pinned his arms. He hissed out, "Despicable Hercules?"

"Yes," I replied.

Death struggled, groaning, trying to thrash about, but he could not free himself from my muscular grasp. "Very well," cried Death, "you have won, son of Zeus. Take her back to Admetus. But some day I shall return for her—and for you!"

"Indeed," I answered, "but not for many years—when Alcestis is old, bent and gray. As for me, I am on my way to immortality and will avoid your chilling, neverending grip." On impulse, I yanked away his cloak, and there I saw—no, it is too monstrous, too frightening to tell. I gave him back the cloak, and an instant later, in an explosion of darkness, the starlight and moonlight momentarily disappearing, he was gone.

I was left now with Alcestis, who remained for a time under Death's spell. I took her chilled hand and nodded to her. "We return to your husband, my friend Admetus."

She nodded from behind her veil, for Death had robbed her temporarily of her voice, and we walked slowly back from the grove toward the city gates, where the sleepy, mourning guards, not noticing the identity of my companion, waved me through.

I had a plan that would, I hoped, surprise and then

amuse Admetus. When I came to his chambers, I stopped and whispered to Alcestis that I wanted her to wait back in the shadows and to stay there till I called her closer. She nodded.

At the door to Admetus' bedroom I called, "Wake up, old friend, I have a surprise for you!"

He rushed to the door, surprised in the first place by my return after my bad-natured leave-taking earlier.

"Hercules!" he said.

"I found out your secret, my friend. Why hadn't you told me of your marriage? Jason's voyage proved good for you and brought you a loving wife. Why did you not tell me that while no relative of yours had died, your wife, your good, sacrificing Alcestis had? Why should your friend Hercules find out second-hand?"

He burst into tears.

I gripped his shoulder and said, "Being that I am your true friend, and hearing of your loss, I went and found you a woman to replace her."

Poor Admetus! This was, I admit, a cruel joke. But I cannot help myself, my sense of humor is a rough-and-tumble sort. He cringed under my hand, convulsed in tears.

He was astounded at my cruelty, but he did not know the great favor, the astounding favor, I had done him which would make right all my teasing. "Come along," I said. "Out here, over there in the shadows, I have brought you a woman just as good as Alcestis ever was."

Admetus, king and warrior, crumpled to the floor in grief. "Please, Hercules," he whimpered, "take her away. You do not understand the love a husband has for his wife."

"Ah," I laughed, "but I do!" I beckoned to Alcestis, and she came forward, but Admetus looked away in agony,

I beckoned to Alcestis, and she came forward,
but Admetus looked away in agony.

thinking I was taunting him with a strange woman. I lifted her veil.

"She's every bit the woman Alcestis was," I declared.

And now my friend Admetus would have struck me,
fed up with my teasing, had not he glanced through his
tears at the lovely face of his wife.

He cried out in joy and embraced her, then me, then
her again. When his tears of joy had ceased to flow, I
told him, "Next time you'll tell me right away and clearly what your troubles are. I have wrestled Death for
you, to retrieve your loving wife. Always know that I am
your friend."

Admetus then tried to convince me to stay and feast,
but I preferred to let them celebrate their reunion
alone. Gathering my goods I set out for distant Thrace.

From Diomedes' four horses I anticipated no special
dangers but their kicking hooves. From Diomedes,
son of the fiercesome god of war Ares, I expected
courtesy, and that he would kindly allow me to run his
horses back to Tiryns to show Eurystheus. How mis-
taken I was!

Diomedes, I learned, was as unnatural a beast as his
horses. When I came to him in his palace and request-
ed the favor of allowing me to borrow his herd, he
called to a servant and said, "Elerion, take Hercules to
the stables and feed the mares."

The young servant turned pale, and begged on his
knees to be let off such an errand. Diomedes grew
angry and shouted, "Go!"

I followed Elerion scarcely knowing what to expect.

We walked out of the palace and across the courtyard to the stables and corral. I saw piles of white
bones in one corner of the corral. Elerion's knees were
knocking, and he was sobbing.

"Horrible!" he muttered, tears in his eyes.

"Why are you troubled?"

"The blood! Poor men! It's shameless! It's wicked, horrid!"

He went behind the stables and returned with a basket of—I can scarcely bring myself to say it—limbs, arms and legs of men!

I was angry at him. I held him and cried, "What is this you are doing?"

"Wicked Diomedes!" he moaned. "He has raised these horses to feast on the flesh of men!"

"Impossible!" I protested.

"No!" he answered. "You must let me do as I was ordered."

I released him and he flung the basket of human limbs over the railings of the corral. The four horses charged over and began to eat, tearing at the flesh.

I could not bring myself to watch any more. Upon my return to the palace, Diomedes mocked me: "Help yourself to my mares, hero! Neither you nor any other man will dare drive such horses across Greece."

"It is wicked and unnatural to alter the god-given tastes of animals," I told him.

"Do not try to frighten me with such claims. The gods have created more monsters than I have done. I have trained my mares as other kings train dogs or birds. They are mine! So just you try to take them with you! They'll eat you alive, son of Zeus!"

My bad temper has never been useful to me. It has destroyed friendships, it has provoked my enemies into harshness. Yet when in response to Diomedes my temper flowed like fire through my blood and into my brain, I did not try to control it. I ran at him and lifted him off his throne. He struck at me with his jeweled staff, but after the first blow I knocked it from his hands. Remember, I had carried boars and lions over my shoulder, a measly king was hardly trouble—especially with the awesome, terrible power my temper seemed to give me.

Diomedes called for his servants, and they all hurried to see what he desired.

"Help me," he cried to the servant Elerion, who was of two minds—duty to the king versus duty to the everlasting gods. He sided with the gods, sensible fellow, and stepped out of my way as I strode out of the palace and crossed the courtyard to the corral. What was I thinking? Perhaps nothing—for a bad temper takes one's mind away.

I arrived at the mares' corral, where they were snorting with a lusty hunger, even after that earlier meal. I raised Diomedes over my head and asked him if he would repent of his brutalization of the horses. He cried out a curse on my head, so I tossed him over the railing into the corral. He screamed for mercy, but I walked away, leaving him to the unnatural appetites of his mares.

I walked back into the palace and called to Elerion, "Where are the bridles? Come with me or not, as you like, as I lead the mares to Tiryns in the Peloponnesus."

"But what of Diomedes?"

"Perhaps he has retrained his mares to be peaceful!" I said grimly. "If not, he is dead, and the mares have had their fill for the day."

The mares, having feasted on bitter-blooded Diomedes, seemed to have lost their strange taste for human flesh. Elerion and I had no trouble driving the gentled horses to Tiryns, though it took several weeks.

9. I Bring Back Hippolyte's Belt and Fight Poseidon's Dragon

EURYSTHEUS WAS as usual distressed to see me alive and well, and the sight of Diomedes' prize horses did not give him joy. They were released and began their long trot back to Thrace.

The king now demanded Hippolyte's belt. You have heard of the Amazons, that tribe of women warriors, the greatest fighters in the world? Hippolyte was their chief, and never had she passed up a chance for a fight. My request for her belt, Eurystheus believed, would bring Amazonian wrath upon my head.

I sailed north for the distant Black Sea, near which the warrior women lived. I did not desire a fight with such difficult opponents, for I was weary of violence and longed for a labor of peace. Had it not been for Hera's hatred of me this labor would have been an easy one.

Upon my arrival on the shore of the Amazons' capital city, Themiscyra, Hippolyte herself came to greet me. I was flattered and greatly pleased and so lay aside all my weaponry in the ship. She was beautiful and as tall as I. Her bearing was that of a dancer, yet she was robed in the skins of wolves and armed with knives, spears and bow and arrows. Her warriors accompanied her to the beach but remained at a respectful distance.

"Hercules," she said, "you honor us by your visit." I

knelt before her and bowed my head. "Tell me your purpose," she continued, "so that I might dismiss my warriors or call them to your aid."

"I do have a purpose," I said. "I have come to ask a favor."

"What favor can we offer the greatest hero of the world?"

"Eurystheus, cruel king in distant Tiryns, requires me in the course of my famous labors to bring him your belt, a prize you collected through warfare."

She did not hesitate. She smiled! Think of a bright sun suddenly breaking through gray clouds. She unfastened her belt, telling me, "Because I so admire your bravery, I give it to you as a gift."

Angry Hera, disguised as one of the Amazonian warriors, shouted, "It's a trick! Look! He means to kill our queen!"

The women, already jealous of Hippolyte's peaceable and tender reception of me, rushed at us just as Hippolyte placed her belt in my hands.

Hippolyte turned to her tribe and commanded them to halt. But Hera raised such a battle cry that no one could hear the queen. She stepped forward, shielding me. She called again to them, but an instant later she cried out in agony, for an arrow meant for me found its mark in her stomach. Her warriors, aghast at this event, ceased their attack and took her from me and tried to revive her. But it was too late—Hera had provoked them into a terrible mistake. Even so, they were angry with me and would have liked to sacrifice me on the funeral pyre of their queen.

From here I sailed away, south through the Bosporus, that strait from the Black Sea which would lead me to the Hellespont, the gate to the Aegean Sea, and my destination of Troy.

I desired to view the newly constructed walls around

the city. Troy sat proudly on the plains of Ilium, on the peninsula of Asia, facing the great continent of Europe and the home of Greeks.

Better for me and for that city that I had not come. Listen to how King Laomedon of Troy, betrayer of men and gods alike, cheated divine Apollo and Poseidon out of their pay when, as an amusement, they joined Laomedon's workers as bricklayers in the building of the famous walls. Imagine those great gods laughing to themselves as they played at the rough chores of common men.

After all, Laomedon had prayed to these very gods for their help, and in disguise they did help him, brick by brick, as if they were men. But at the end of their labor, Laomedon, not knowing them for gods, threatened to whip them like dogs should they insist on their wages.

Outraged, they flew off to Olympos. From there, when the wall was completed, Apollo hurled a plague down upon the city while Poseidon, lord of the sea, smacked the walls with a tremendous tidal wave and then left a dragon at the beach. Priests of Apollo and Poseidon came to Laomedon, telling him that the plague would stop and the dragon go away only if he would sacrifice his darling, beautiful daughter, Hesione, to Poseidon's monster.

This Laomedon agreed to do, and on a rock just out into the sea he left her—she weeping, yet a willing sacrifice for her father's crime. On the very day she was delivered and bound to the rock, I came to Troy. Told of the events, I declared my intentions of saving blameless Hesione. Conniving Laomedon, seeing another chance to gain in spite of his folly, encouraged me, assuring me that should I kill the dragon and rescue Hesione, he would award me a golden vine, shaped and created by the fire god Hephaestos himself.

I rushed to the shore and saw in the distance Poseidon's immense dragon making its way through the waters toward Hesione. Although I was fully dressed and outfitted with my sword, I leapt into the water, swimming toward the rock where Hesione was

I clamped the sword between my teeth as I swam to Hesione, arriving an instant before the dragon.

bound. With one hand grasping the sword, I was swimming hardly fast enough. So, just as a sailor will grip his knife between his teeth to keep his hands free, I clamped the sword between my teeth as I swam the final length, arriving an instant before the dragon.

This monster breathed fire, but its swimming and the splashing waves had momentarily doused his flame. I had little time to lose before he struck, so I cut the ropes that bound lovely Hesione and shouted to her, "Swim for the shore, maiden—and do not look back."

She gave me one sweet look of gratitude before she dove in. The dragon was about to give chase or rear its head and send a burst of fire after her when, in a surprisingly reckless turn of mind, even for me, I leaped into the dragon's mouth. The Augean stables were sweeter to me than the rank, burning smell within the dragon's belly. For two days or three I attacked the dragon from within, while it desperately swam through the oceans. I must have destroyed his will or ability to swim, because he beached himself near Ilium. My sword, that gleaming gift from Hermes, finally cut through the dragon's scaly thick skin, and I found myself on the very shore of Troy. The hair on my head and face were gone, but I was not too much the worse for wear. I marched across the plains of Ilium to Troy's walls. Who greeted me? Who raised a shout in my honor? No one!

The guards at one gate called out to me, "Please, Hercules, do not kill us for refusing you entrance. King Laomedon does not want to see you again. He says you are to go away."

"What of my reward?"

"He changed his mind. He said the golden vine is worth a dozen of his daughters."

"I'll go," I said to the guards, "but tell your master I'll be back before long to destroy Troy."

That same day I left for Tiryns to deliver up Hippolyte's belt to Eurystheus.

10. The Monster Geryon and His Beautiful Cattle

AFTER HE took one admiring look at Hippolyte's belt, Eurystheus cursed me and tossed it aside. His darling daughter, Odetia, spotted the belt and in the way of little girls dressed herself in it. Eurystheus, on seeing the girl imitating an Amazon, smiled. For one moment he seemed to have the feelings that make a man decent. Then he turned away, put her out of his mind and let his usual severity take over.

"Hercules, I return you to your capture of animals, since such tasks seem to suit you. Go to the western ocean, the edge of the world, and bring me the monster Geryon's cattle, those lovely grazers in the land of sunsets, and bring them safely back."

I was not tired of traveling and enjoying adventures. And so if Eurystheus wanted me at the greatest distance he knew of on earth, I would make the best of it. Had I sailed from Tiryns to Erytheia, the southern point of Europe, this labor would not have taken more than a half-year. As it was I set out sailing westward, but on an impulse landed on the southern side of the Mediterranean, in Libya. It was there, on the northern tip of Africa, so close to Europe, that I borrowed a stone-cutter's tools and spent a week or two shaping a boulder into a massive pillar. It was not an artful job. However, I was content with its size, a towering monument to myself and the farthest reach so far of my journeys. I hired a team of oxen to drag it with me to the cliffs that overlook the sea's passage from the Mediterranean to the unknown western ocean beyond. With all the strength the oxen and I could muster, we upraised the massive pillar of stone.

For two or three moments I gazed in admiration at it, but when I glanced across the straits to Europe I understood that one pillar would hardly do. I dismissed the hardworking oxen and rushed down to the straits, where I plunged into the water and swam for the other side. The ocean beyond seemed to desire me, pulling on my arms and legs, but I would not relent and swam with hard strokes until I arrived at land.

As on the African side I borrowed a stone-cutter's tools and carved myself a similar tower of stone. This time, however, the stone I elected to carve was lying on the very spot where I wished to post it. Raising it, however, was difficult, causing even me to strain and almost despair. Let me thank the god Apollo who, without my knowing at the time, put his shoulder into my effort. In a matter of moments, after hours of my pushing and grunting, the pillar rose, a companion to the one on the opposite side. The Pillars of Hercules, marking the edge of the western world, could be seen for many miles, from land and sea.

From the straits it was a short distance to the land of Geryon, the odd monster who resembled three men joined at one waist. So many arms, so many legs! With such a supply I could scarcely have kept myself from tripping, but Geryon made the most of his extra limbs. He owned thousands of cattle and was king of this western land. But king of what? There were few people and for them he scarcely cared. He loved only his cattle, tended by a servant named Eurytion and the monstrous two-headed dog Orthros.

I climbed the low mountains where I saw the cattle grazing and sat there awaiting Geryon, hoping he would allow me to take one of his many herds. Instead, Orthros found me. I stood up while Eurytion, that vicious man, ordered the dog to attack me. I had no intention of harming the dog, but its snapping jaws left me no choice. I swung my club at him, and the dog yelped but refused to give up the fight. When Eurytion sent a spear at me, I returned fire with my bow and arrow, killing him and the monstrous dog.

I now decided to take the cattle without asking leave of Geryon. After all, his own man and dog had attacked me without cause. But I had no sooner crossed a river with a herd of his finest bulls and cows when Geryon set out after me. He was not in the mood to make a deal or talk. He sent a half-dozen spears flying after me. I raised my shield just in time to deflect the death they intended.

I hardly knew where to let loose an arrow in return, there were so many of him! I aimed left, then right, then center, wondering which part of him to dispose of first. Then I saw the folly of attacking the edges of a one-man army. I aimed at his center, his vulnerable waist, and my shot hit its mark.

One arrow and Geryon sprawled dead in a heap of arms and legs!

After I had driven the cattle through the Iberian peninsula, Iolaos met me and we ventured on a long trek through the strange wild lands of Europe. I joined in many contests against arrogant men who thought they could outfight or outwrestle me and I outwitted countless robbers and bandits.

11. The End of My Labors

AS MUCH as Eurystheus dreaded me, he had come to expect my successful return. In the long stretch I had been away he had come up with the most taxing of all my labors.

"Very well," he greeted me, seeing Geryon's cattle in the courtyard, "I wish you to make another long journey. Fetch me, if you are able, a few of the apples of the Hesperides."

"As you like," I said. "But where are they?"

Eurystheus smiled, saying, "I have no idea. Part of your task will be to find out."

So I set out, aimless, and praying to the gods for guidance. Athene herself descended from Olympos and told me, "The Hesperides are known as the Daughters of Evening, they are lovely nymphs who tend the golden apple tree. At night, look to the west, where you can see the Hesperides shining as stars. Below them you will find the tree. Beware, brave Hercules, this tree is guarded from intruders by a loathsome, lava-spouting snake."

"So again I am off to the edge of the western world!" I laughed. At night I watched the stars and by day I sailed by their guidance for western Libya.

It was in Libya that I met King Antaeus, that unfriendly son of Gaia, our great Mother Earth. What a cruel man! Where other kings greet strangers with food and drink and engage them in conversation, Antaeus would challenge his would-be guests to a wrestling match.

This match, win or lose, did not end with a feast but

always with death, the death of the stranger, for Antaeus would kill the weary man at first opportunity. That I was the son of Zeus and famed throughout the world for my strength made no impression on him. "Out here," he said, "we do not receive much news. I've never heard of you, and I don't care a hoot who your father is. Let us wrestle, Hermeles, or whatever your name is."

"*Hercules!*" I shouted. He laughed, and my anger stormed within me.

The keys to wrestling are strength and balance, and Antaeus seemed to have a full complement of both. I could not understand, however, why after I managed to throw him to the ground he would regain his strength— indeed, find more strength than he had had!

I am not a watchful man, but I noticed, once, as he and I circled each other, grabbing out at the other's arms, that he pretended to slip. He fell to the ground and suddenly bounded up rejuvenated! He ran at me and knocked me off my feet.

The hard ground hardly lifted my spirits, but when I looked with shame at the dirt on my hands, an idea dawned on me. I got to my feet and planned my next move. Antaeus rushed again at me, but this time instead of tumbling into the dirt with him, I pulled his waist close against my chest and lifted him off the ground. Take the air from a flame and watch the fire disappear. Just so, taking Antaeus away from contact with his mother made his strength disappear. It was Earth who gave him renewed vigor. I wrapped my arms around Antaeus, finally even crossing my forearms behind his back, while Antaeus, desperate man, pushed against my face with his right hand and pushed against my shoulder with the other. His feet stretched and strained to touch Mother Earth.

Without his mother Antaeus was just another man! I crushed the murderer of innocent strangers in my arms. Then I left him on the ground, where his mother, I presume, covered him and gave him proper burial.

I continued through Libya until I reached the end of the world. There at the world's edge stands mighty Atlas, that Titan who has the weight of the sky on his shoulders. Without him the sky would fall upon us all! This task he must perform because long ago he fought in league with the other Titans against Zeus and the Olympians.

Beside him lay the walled gardens of the lovely Hesperides. I greeted the Titan, and said, "I am Hercules."

Atlas nodded but did not otherwise reply.

"I have come in quest of the golden apples."

Atlas, his voice deep and rough with strain, said, "They're just over there in the lovely nymphs' garden. (Grunt!) Go look."

I peeked over the high wall of the paradise and saw a snake the size of a dragon guarding the apple tree, above which the Hesperides were lightly dancing. I have never passed up a challenge, but if by my wits I was able to avoid death or injury, I tried to use them. I said, gazing up at the blue sky, "You bear a large weight, Titan."

"Tremendous," he said, "a tremendous weight."

"Perhaps, mighty Atlas, you would like a rest from your duty? Say, what if I held up the sky for you while you went in and picked me some apples?"

Atlas frowned, and said, "Is this a trick?"

"I? How could I trick you?"

"I don't know. I don't wholly trust you, Hercules, but all right, a few moments of rest would do me well. Yes, I agree (grunt!), I'll do you a service as you do me one."

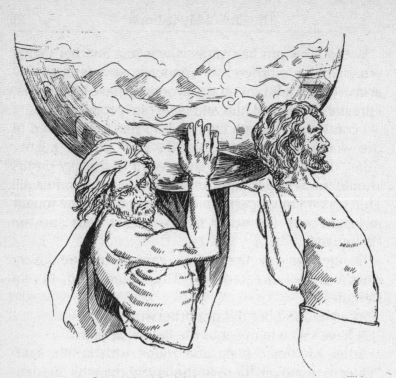

*I stood beside Atlas as he stooped and
lowered the sky onto my shoulders.*

I stood beside him as he stooped and lowered the sky onto my shoulders, though I must give thanks to Athene, who, at the last instant, invisibly took some of the weight upon her upraised right hand.

Atlas, relieved of his chore, let out a deep breath, stretched his arms out, straightened his back and said, "Thank you, Hercules. I needed a break."

"The apples," I muttered, my jaw clenched with strain.

Atlas laughed. "The dragon's no problem for me," he said. He picked off a flower that grew outside the wall and hopped over. This flower, I learned, was a charm that lulled the snake to sleep. Not very much later, Atlas hopped back over the wall. He was carrying an armful of apples.

"See?" he said. "If you know how to do things, they're easy." He set the apples down and was at my side, about to take back his burden, when an idea came to him. He straightened up and clapped me on the shoulder. "My friend, my mighty little friend Hercules," he said, "you are bearing up very well!"

"Very well!" I repeated, but my shoulders were very strained.

"You are doing such a good job in my stead," he went on, "what if we trade places for a year or two?"

Invisible Athene's wisdom, whispered into my ear, kept me calm, and I replied, "Very well, Titan. It's no trouble to me. The exercise will do me good, in fact. But, please, wait a moment. Before you go away, would you mind holding the sky for two moments while I find a pillow to lay across my head and shoulders?"

Atlas laughed, saying proudly, "I myself have never needed a cushion! It's not strictly proper, but I pity you, so, all right, go get yourself a thick pad of some sort." Atlas reshouldered the burden and I stepped out from under the sky.

I let out a sigh of relief. "Thank you, Atlas," I said. I bent over and began to collect the apples he had picked.

"But you're staying here!" cried Atlas. "You won't need those."

"Farewell!" I said.

Atlas stamped his foot at me, but without another to shoulder his burden he could not chase me. Athene flew off to Olympos, and I began the long journey back to Tiryns.

Those apples were so glorious Eurystheus was almost pleased I returned.

The final labor, however, was meant to do away with me. Few men have ever gone to Hades, home of the dead, and returned alive. That was the destination Eurystheus gave me, with the task of fetching the hideous three-headed watchdog of the underworld, Cerberos.

Without the guidance of goddess Athene I could not have sailed across the distant seas and found the secret underworld entrance. She commanded the ship and we had the best of weather and winds. How many long weeks was it that we sailed? We came to a rocky island that resembled so many others and landed. Not far ashore there was a wide-mouthed cave, from which we heard terrible twitterings; these were the voices, she told me, of the newly dead. She led me by the hand to the entrance, where fearsome Cerberos was about to raise a din with his triple-tongued barking. Instead, seeing Athene's owlish divine eyes, he cowered and let us pass.

With us safely within the outer reaches of Hades, Athene stopped and touched my right shoulder. "Here it is that I must stop. Clever Hercules, you must convince Hades, lord of the underworld, of your need to borrow Cerberos."

I wandered down the winding cave into the dusky land of the dead, where I saw the smoky spirits of those who had lived; they were squeaking like bats, and twitchily flitting about. I shuddered, then proceeded until I found my way to the throne room of Lord Hades himself.

"Well, well, well," laughed Hades, who did not have a warm laugh at all. "My brother Zeus's son has come to pay his respects to his uncle."

"All respect the dead, Hades. For though we all fear death, it gives our bodies peace."

"Yes, yes, so it is said," Hades answered impatiently. "What is it you want of me?"

"I ask permission to take your dog to Tiryns."

Again Hades laughed his cold, unfriendly laugh. "Go right ahead, nephew, by all means. But the rules are these: use no club or other weapon to make him follow you."

That, of course, left me with my hands. I pulled my lion-skin cloak tight over my body and when I finished the long and winding way to the entrance, I got down on all fours and crept up on the keen-eyed dog. He had never seen such a strange beast! Just as his heads began to bark in warning, I sprang like the lion in whose skin I was wrapped. Cerberos could not bite through

Cerberos followed me onto the ship, and I leashed him before walking into the king's court.

my Nemean cloak, and we wrestled for some time. Finally, he grew tired, and as with any dog that knows it has been conquered, he rolled over, showing his belly. I laughed, and when I petted him, the gentle monster, he licked my masterful hands. Cerberos followed me away from the gloomy underworld and onto the ship. Athene was not with us, but her guidance seemed to fill my head. It did not seem long before we had crossed the seas and returned to Tiryns. To keep Cerberos from tearing after the men of the city, I leashed him before walking into the king's court.

At the sight of him, Eurystheus cried, "Take him away!" So frightened was he that he jumped again into the tall jar beside his throne. How keenly Hades' dog and I longed for Eurystheus' death! He popped out his head for an instant and screamed, "Leave me alone, cousin! You have performed your labors. Now go, and never let me see you again!"

Oh, how I laughed. I led Cerberos over to the throne, and we peeked into the jar. "Farewell, wicked man!" I called. "May Cerberos soon enjoy the sight of you in his own home." Then I led Hades' dog away with a simple "Here, boy!" We were on the seas for only a night. The gods must have seen to our passage. When I awoke, the ship had landed and Cerberos was hopping over the side to sniff at the entrance of his cave.

I slept on the anchored boat that night, but when I awoke, Dawn had come with her rosy fingers, and I was lying under a blanket on the ship, which was docked now outside Eurystheus' palace.

12. My Revenge on Troy and My Fight Alongside the Gods

"IS LABOR its own reward?" I wondered. I had successfully performed twelve tasks, but no thunder, no shouts of triumph sprang from the gods. I was greeted, instead, by the sounds of the world: creaky carts passing by, common birds chirping and fluttering. "Zeus, my father?" I prayed, gazing upward. "Am I to continue living on earth?" There was no sign, no reply, and I spent my first day walking through the countryside. What was to come of my hard-earned divinity? It was not in the haystack in which I tucked myself that night, and from which I was cautiously roused in the morning by a poor farmer's young son.

"Big man," I heard as if in a dream.

I opened one eye, the straw poking into my face, and saw a curly-haired little child. His curly hair was blond, his eyes the swirling green of the shallow sea off Thessaly. "Wake up," the boy said.

"Athene?" I asked, for she so liked to disguise herself as beautiful children or youths.

"Me not Tina," he said. "Me Maxion."

"Fetch me water, then, Maxie."

The boy left and returned with his father, who brandished a hoe, while trying to keep his boy far behind him. The man was shaking, his knees knocking, and his voice trembled as he said, "Are you a god—or the thief who steals my hens?"

Extending my hand in friendship, I laughed. "I'm not one or the other, I'm only a man like yourself."

"In that case," he said, glancing nervously over his shoulder, "let me offer you a portion of bread and cheese, and as much water as you need."

"Thank you, kind farmer, but tell me of your thief."

"I would if I could, but I can't, so I shan't. We've not seen him, or heard him, only found little piles of bones on cold pits of burned wood."

"In return for your hospitality, I'll catch your thief, farmer. If it takes me a day or two, I hope you won't mind."

"Not at all—and should you succeed, kind prince (for you must be the son of a great king), I'll offer you the best eggs you've ever tasted."

I caught the thief that night, a neighbor it turned out, who had been jealous of the farmer's very modest success. In my grasp the thief confessed all and turned over to his victim a fat pig, more than recompense, in my mind, for the crime, yet hardly fair enough, thought the farmer. In truth, the farmer's eggs were hardly better than any others I have tasted, but I thanked him well and told him Zeus, god of goodwill toward strangers, would bless his home.

Now I itched to take care of my own business. A servant performs chores all day for his master, then, if he is lucky, returns to his hovel and prepares his own supper, and with a spare moment stares at the dancing flames of his little fire. Just so was I left to my own tasks now that I was free of Eurystheus' ill will.

I wished to settle scores with the king of Troy, Laomedon. I visited the kingdoms of several friends, declaring my intentions of revenge. I repeat now what I told the king of Salamis, Telamon, one of my former mates on the *Argo*.

"You honor me, Telamon, by celebrating my fabulous labors. I thank you for your gifts and abundant praises. You may be surprised to hear that I beg a favor of you— I'll go straight to the point—I ask for fifty of your finest men and the best ship. I'll keep no secrets; I mean to attack and burn Troy." I went on to tell him what you already know, about how Laomedon refused to pay what he promised when I saved his daughter Hesione from Poseidon's sea dragon.

Telamon readily agreed to help me, and he became my second-in-command over six ships of three hundred fierce and hardy warriors, volunteers from his and the other kingdoms friendly to my mission.

We sailed for Troy in early spring. Upon arrival I assembled the forces on the beach, and then decided to give Laomedon one more chance to fulfill his promise. I walked alone to the walls of Troy, at the base of which I called up to the cowering soldiers and said, "Hand over my reward for saving Hesione, that golden vine designed by Hephaestos, godly master of fire, and I'll leave you in peace."

Laomedon, peeking over the wall, and then hurling a long spear in my direction, cried out, "There's your reward, Muscle-Man!"

I reached out and caught the spear in midair, and then broke it over my knee. I walked back to the ships, and Telemon and I directed the attack.

When you hear how, in the generation after mine, it took the armies of great Achilles, Agamemnon and Odysseus ten years to defeat Troy, marvel at our deed! It took us one day! Laomedon attacked us on the plains with thousands of his men. They knew they were fighting for their lives, but the gods gave us victory. We turned them back, and they retreated into the city. Then we smashed at their walls with battering rams.

Brave Telamon's crew broke through before mine had and, I admit, this caused me envy—a serpent whose poison is more dangerous than the hydra's. Telamon climbed into the breach in the wall and was about to take the honor of being the first enemy within the city. He turned and saw me, my face hard with anger and resentment. He quickly jumped back and fell to his knees and began piling rocks in a mound.

"What do you mean by this?" I roared at him, my temper flashing lightning from my eyes.

"I mean," he said, wise diplomat, "to make an altar to Troy's conquerer—you, great Hercules!"

My rage evaporating like steam, I laughed at his cleverness. "Thank you, Telamon, for granting me this honor." I climbed through the breach and other soldiers followed.

Once our army was within the walls, Laomedon stood no chance. We defeated him and his soldiers. Telamon, as a reward from me, was allowed to marry beautiful Hesione.

Remember Hera's hatred? Though I had succeeded in my labors, she still wanted trouble for me. As I sailed with my mates from our successful devastation of Troy, she sent terrible storms down upon us, which would have buried us in watery graves had not Zeus punished her and given us sudden fine weather.

When we were safe again, and had celebrated our victory over Troy and the storms, I lay upon the deck of the ship one evening. The warm breeze soothed me; the stars were blinking high above. Then, mysteriously, it was not stars blinking above me but the divine face of Athene.

Her eyes glowed, but no other sailor could see her. She spoke, but no other sailor could hear her.

"Hercules, so wondrous are you, even the gods admire you. I come this time not to give aid but to ask for it. We gods on Olympos face an attack from the terrible, monstrous Giants, those enormous children of Earth and Sky. We know from signs we have read in the stars that without your help we will be conquered. Help us, as many of us have helped you."

"I will do all in my power, wise Athene, for the Olympians are my friends and protectors." After I had gathered my weapons, we ascended in her chariot, flying west to the plains near Phlegra's volcanos. It was pitch dark there, unlit, on Zeus's orders, by the sun, moon or stars.

The battle which followed, so important to the continued sovereignty of the Olympian gods, was hardly witnessed, even by its participants. Here and there, of course, the flash of Zeus's lightning brought the scene of destruction to our eyes.

With steady light the Giants might have found the earthly plant that would give them their sought-after immortality—a state of being which would have meant everlasting war, or, at best, an unhappy compromise of power.

In the darkness we saw with our other senses. When Athene, great warrior, set out after the Giant Enceladus, she pursued the sound of his heavy footsteps, which must have caused earthquakes throughout Europe. She then mustered all her colossal strength and lifted a mountain range that one of Zeus's thunderbolts had loosened, and hurled it end over end in Enceladus' direction. Sharp-eared, she had heard his frantic splashing in the southern sea. The mountain range found its mark, crushing the Giant into the sea depths. Do you know the island of Sicily? It sits even today atop the brutal Giant.

For my part, I assisted in several killings, shooting an arrow through one eye of a Giant while Apollo, master of archery, fixed the other eye with a winged dart. Were we shooting blindly? No, even in the darkness, the light of life shone in the Giants' eyes, while we, more clever, narrowed our eyes.

My proudest moment in the war with the Giants was dispatching Alcyoneus, the strongest of them all. In the land where he was born, Pallene in Chaldice, where we were fighting, he was immortal. Beast! He must have been as tall as an ancient tree. I took aim at the glint of his right eye, and when he fell, shaking the earth, his hands busily covering his wound, I pounced. Lions will drag their prey for miles until they find a peaceful place to eat it. I dragged Alcyoneus a dozen miles, until we were beyond the confines of life-giving Pallene.

What is it about our homelands that gives us life? I do not know, but within moments of his transplantation from Pallene, Alcyoneus' torturing wound killed him.

My great father Zeus disposed of many Giants with his thunderbolts, but let me give credit as well to the huntress Artemis, swift Hermes, crooked-legged Hephaestos and Poseidon, lord of the seas. Notice that I do not mention Hera, for she, though willing enough to fight alongside her fellow Olympians, was being punished by Zeus for her attack on me.

The war with the Giants done with, I was returned to my life of suffering, of which I shall tell more in the following chapter.

13. My Marriage, Death and Immortal Life

AFTER THE fight with the Giants I decided to retire and live in peace until such time as the gods would have me live with them on Olympos. Why is it that what we most desire is the last thing we obtain?

Oeneus was king of Calydon in Aetolia, that western reach of mainland Greece. He treated me as a friend and as the famed hero I was. For his part, he was famous for his hospitality, regularly hosting a boar hunt in which great men throughout Greece participated. But what I longed for, and for a short time enjoyed, was peace: days without war, a lack of desire to travel, a contented spirit. But can a man in love with a woman who is wooed by another man ever be at peace?

For the first week or two I lived within Oeneus' palace, so pleasant was it that I scarcely thought of the better life to come on Olympos. I was well-fed and well-entertained. Oeneus and his wife, Althaea, were all that they should have been in their attentions to my comfort. And yet I detected unhappiness in Althaea.

"Kind queen," I said one day, "what troubles you? The king is well, is he not?"

"Yes, he is well."

"And your children, delightful children, sure to be heroes or queens in their time, they are well?"

"Yes, they are well—but one, she who will marry soon, is not happy."

"Which one of them is to marry, and why is she unhappy?"

"You have not seen her, Hercules. Lovely Deianira has hidden herself away. Her intended husband is Achelous, the god of the swiftly flowing river that divides our country from Acarnania. When he presents himself to her he appears in the form of a river or of a bull or of a snake with gemlike scales or sometimes as a man—but even then his face is bull-like, with a mouth scarcely able to contain the river water within him.— He is a god, Hercules, and no man in Aetolia dares to approach my daughter and ask for her hand. Achelous would surely kill him."

That, then, was the end of my peace! What emotion ever caused more fights than love? Aphrodite denies it, but I swear that as gentle Althaea led me to the roof of the palace, where I was shown the sight of Deianira weeping in a small garden far below, I felt a prick of my skin—the arrow of reckless Cupid that sent the poison of love coursing through my veins. Hydra's poison hardly works faster or more painfully than Love's.

What could I see? A sad but beautiful young woman, her long brown hair piled atop her head and decorated with yellow and blue flowers. The gold bangles on her wrists chimed when she raised her hands to hide those tender weeping eyes.

"Hercules!" exclaimed Althaea, shaking me by the shoulder. "I see Love has transfixed you, but I warn you, do not attempt to fight Achelous for my daughter. Better to allow her to pray for her death before she weds such a terrifying god as Achelous than for you to endanger yourself!"

Even had I not been struck with love for Deianira I could not have allowed her to marry against her will. "When does Achelous pay his next visit?" I asked.

"Why," said Althaea, "please, Hercules, do not think of challenging him! You came here for peace, not to further your heroic deeds! It does not matter that this is the very day Achelous comes to claim her as his wife."

As I recall these moments I do not know whether it was Aphrodite's spell or Althaea's—she who so easily led me by the nose —that brought on the end of my mortal life.

"I declare myself a suitor for Deianira's hand in marriage," I told Althaea. "If Deianira prefers me and Achelous will not accept her choice, then he and I must fight for the right to be her husband."

"I'm sure I cannot dissuade you from such a noble action, dear Hercules, and so I will not try," said Althaea.

From where we stood upon the palace roof, we heard the bellowing of a bull. Within moments we heard the rush of a river of water and a tremendous splash against the palace gates.

"It's Achelous!" cried Althaea.

When we arrived in the main hall below, there slithered an enormous, brilliantly flashing snake, Achelous yet again, his forked tongue hissing words to Oeneus: "Yes, I have come for your sweet daughter. She will be the supreme queen of Aetolia's greatest river."

"She does not want to marry you!" cried out Althaea. "She prefers the hero Hercules."

"Hercules!" spat the snake, transforming before our eyes into a fountain of water. He addressed me, his bubbling voice gushing out, "Son of Zeus, do not interfere. I saw Deianira first, and I want her for my own. If you stand in my way I will be forced to fight you."

"You would marry this woman against her will?" I said.

He did not reply except to rise in a towering wave and splash down upon me. In a few moments I was washed out of the palace and down into the meadow nearby. There, as a spangled serpent, he sprang out of the grass and wrapped his coils around me, crushing the breath out of me, nearly breaking my ribs. I grabbed for his neck and in return tried squeezing the breath out of him. Suddenly, however, he burst into the shape of a tremendous bull. He pushed me down, snorting steam, and then, thinking to gore me, swung his head.

I grabbed those horns and lifted him off his bullish feet. To my surprise one of the horns broke off, and Achelous fell to the ground, where he now resembled a bull-faced, dribble-mouthed man.

He angrily got up, snatched the horn from me and tried to replant it on his head. When it fell to the ground he snorted and said, "Very well, Hercules, you win. I mean never again to fight for the love of a mortal woman."

He departed and before the day was through he had resumed his watery way.

I, on the other hand, became the proud husband of lovely Deianira. I had entered, however, the final phase of my life. Why is it that Deianira and I could not live together for decades as happily as we were those first months and years?

I blame myself, for just as some men are made for love, others are made for work or for war. A terrible accident, wherein I killed a lad, led my father-in-law Oeneus to exile me. One evening while I was in the midst of telling of one of my adventures, I swung my hand violently to demonstrate a wrestling move I had tried on Antaeus. I did not know that a serving boy was standing beside me. I knocked him down, and his head hit the stone floor. I leapt out of my chair to comfort him, but he soon died.

Feeling myself to be guilty, I agreed to my father-in-law's custom of exiling murderers, and with Deianira and our son, Hyllos, moved north to Trachis in Thessaly.

It was during our journey to Trachis that the end of my life occurred. At the river Evenus, where we stood on the bank pondering what course to take, a sly-looking centaur greeted us. "Need a lift?" he asked, winking unpleasantly at Deianira. He knew who I was, for I had done battle with Nessos' clansmen many years before when he and his brothers had attacked me and Pholos in that centaur's cave. I did not, to my regret, remember him. He commanded a small raft, which he offered as transportation across the river's swift currents. There was room enough for Deianira and our child but not for me. I would swim.

I dove into the swift river and stroked hard against the heavy current. Nessos, however, let the raft float quickly downstream. In no time at all he would have kidnapped Deianira and my child, bringing them to his lair in the mountains.

I, meanwhile, having made my way across the river, looked back and could hardly see the centaur's raft. I called out, "Where are you going with my wife and child?"

In response Nessos cackled and waved good-bye. He was nearly at a bend in the river, after which point I might not have found him among the numerous forks the fast river took. I strung my bow, pulled out an arrow and let it fly!

The hydra-poisoned arrow struck the centaur in the chest, and he fell wounded, and Deianira directed the raft to the river's edge.

What happened next I learned later, after I arrived on Olympos:

"Forgive me," said Nessos to Deianira.

"How can I?" said she.

"Listen," Nessos continued, "and take this wool." The centaur took from a bag about his neck some wool, which unbeknownst to Deianira, he smeared with his own newly poisoned blood. "Weave from it a robe for your husband. It contains a charm. Once he wears it, he will never leave you for other adventures or wives."

Deianira, though doubting the wicked centaur, took the wool and hid it away. I had promised to live with her and our child in peace and comfort, but she knew my nature better than I did, and half-expected me to break my promise. This potion, she thought, would preserve our love.

Nessos died before I reached the raft. Deianira told me nothing of the centaur's words. We continued on our way.

Not long after we settled in Trachis, I heard of an archery contest in Oechalia, to the west. I could not resist the desire to join in; after all, what man could match my skill with the bow? The thought of men of lesser talent winning a prize that belonged to me preyed on my mind. Deianira noticed my restlessness.

"A spirit is pulling at you, my husband."

"Not a spirit, my wife, but a contest."

"Oh?"

"King Eurytos of Oechalia invites the skilled archers of Greece to compete for a prize."

"You long to go?"

I admitted that I did.

"Then go," she said. "You will be miserable if you do not."

Better had she scolded me! I did go, and I did win the prize—the hand of Eurytos' daughter, Iole! I desired no woman but my wife, but how was I to refuse the honor done me? I was gone several weeks. Deianira, poor woman, heard about the results of the contest and grew despondent. She thought she had lost me to the world and to another woman.

I was standing near the fiery altar when the hydra's poison in the robe melted and began eating away at my flesh.

It was not so; I did not care for Iole. Rather, I was building an altar to my father, lord Zeus. When I sent back a messenger to ask Deianira for a ceremonial robe in which I could perform my prayers, she believed I was coolly preparing for a wedding to Iole. She remembered Nessos' gift, and after some hesitation, wove the wool into a long, beautiful white garment for me, with which the messenger returned.

As the messenger held the robe up for me to see, I admired Deianira's fine work. Then, ignorant of the terrors the next moments would hold, I let the messenger drape the garment over my shoulders. I was standing in front of the fiery altar, breathing incense and thanking Zeus for my life on earth, when the hydra's poison within the robe melted and dripped like hot wax onto my skin! I roared in pain, and yet when I tried to tear off the robe, it dissolved into me, eating away at my flesh. Such agony I would not wish on Eurystheus!

Lord Zeus saw that this was the end of my mortal life and so he gathered dense, purifying clouds over his suffering son. At the sound of a deafening thunderclap, I disappeared off the face of the earth and arrived on Mount Olympos. I became immortal! Even Hera, my old enemy, now admired me. She took me in her arms and kissed me.

"Hercules," she said, "you are every bit as worthy as I to live on Olympos. Please forgive the trials I put you through. But, after all, you have arrived at your destiny. To prove to you that I mean you no harm and bear love for you, I offer in marriage my daughter Hebe, the goddess of youth."

"Noble Hera, I forgive you and accept your offer to marry beautiful immortal Hebe. I am honored to be in your presence and among the Olympians."

Forever after have I lived on Mount Olympos among the gods!